To Patricia,

Thanks for your ... ter.
I consider it a great honor
to have been asked to speak
at the AACN.

I hope that you enjoy
"Smile...!" and find it
interesting, as well as
informative.

I wish you the very best.

Sincerely,
Tex

Smile ...
or I'll Kick
Your Bed!

Smile ...
or I'll Kick
Your Bed!

TEX GOEN, Jr., M.D.

W·W·NORTON & COMPANY

New York · London

THE TEXT *of this book is composed in photocomposition Electra. Display type is Trump Medieval and Perpetua. Manufacturing is by the Maple-Vail Book Manufacturing Group. Book design is by Marjorie J. Flock.*

Library of Congress Cataloging in Publication Data
Goen, Tex, Jr. (M.D.)
    Smile . . . or I'll kick your bed!
      1. Aortocoronary bypass—Complications and sequelae.
      2. Aortocoronary bypass—Psychological aspects.
    I. Title.
RD598.G59   617'.412   80–20223

ISBN 0–393–01433–9

W. W. Norton & Company, Inc. 500 Fifth Avenue, New York, N.Y. 10110
W. W. Norton & Company Ltd. 25 New Street Square, London EC4A 3NT

2 3 4 5 6 7 8 9 0

To Sylvia, Monte, and Gary

ILLUSTRATIONS, PAGES 26, 27, 28, 31, 65, 67, and 169.

GLOSSARY, PAGE 187.

Introduction

MORE THAN one-half of the people who die in the United States this year will do so from heart and blood-vessel-related diseases. The vast majority of these deaths will be from heart attack. Odds are that you or some member of your family have already faced this problem or will in the future.

Fifteen years ago there was little that could be done surgically to treat people suffering from these diseases. The subsequent development of the coronary artery vein bypass procedure changed this situation dramatically. Now, patients with coronary artery disease that has progressed to a stage unresponsive to medications have an acceptable alternative that can greatly improve the quality of their lives. This alternative is open-heart surgery, where a vein is taken from the leg to bypass the blocked heart arteries.

In the past, open-heart surgery was associated with a significant mortality. The more complex the procedure, the higher the risk. There was even a time when internists and cardiologists were reluctant to send a patient to surgery because of this high mortality rate. Only when their patients had deteriorated to a point where heart surgery was a last resort were they willing to recommend it. The results in these cases were even more dismal. Consequently, the mere mention of the words *open-heart surgery* struck fear in any patient who faced this possibility.

Initially the only candidates for open-heart surgery were children with congenital (birth) defects of the heart and adults with leakages or narrowings of the heart valves. But it was not until 1967 that an operation was developed that would help people with blockages in the heart arteries. This surgical procedure involved taking a vein from the leg and using it to directly bypass the blockages. Suddenly, almost overnight, there was a dramatic increase in the number of candidates for open-heart surgery.

By the early 1970s heart surgery was no longer confined to the large medical centers. The coronary artery bypass procedure was being performed in many large community hospitals throughout the country on a daily basis. The rapid influx of new young surgeons into the field of cardiovascular (heart and blood vessel) surgery, working alongside well-established heart surgeons, resulted in a massive outpouring of new ideas and technology. There were rapid advances in the heart-lung machine, monitoring systems, anesthetic agents, and artificial valves. Even more important, new techniques were developed for preserving and protecting the heart muscle while it was stopped without its critical blood supply. The inevitable outcome was a rapid decline in mortality as the state of the art improved. Today most open-heart operations can be performed with a death rate that is less than 8 to 10 percent. The mortality rate of the coronary artery bypass procedure, in the usual uncomplicated case, is around 2 to 3 percent. This is not too different from the risks of removing a gall bladder or resecting part of the stomach for ulcer disease.

It has become obvious to me that approximately 5 percent of the patients who undergo coronary artery bypass surgery do extremely well post-operatively on their own. They are able to return to full employment and do all the things that they hoped they would be able to do following surgery. They do very well because of self-motivation. It does not matter who performs their surgery or where it is done.

At the other end of the spectrum, approximately 5 percent of the patients who undergo this operation will do very poorly post-operatively. This group of patients lacks inner motivation. They will most likely never return to work, will have multiple complaints the rest of their lives, and will essentially be "emotional cripples" after heart surgery.

This book is directed to the 90 percent of patients who are between these two extremes. If this large percentage of patients receives the proper pre-operative guidance and preparation so that they understand fully the risks and possible benefits of coronary artery bypass surgery—or any other type of surgery, for that matter—knowing what is expected of them and what they should expect from themselves, then they will do well also. They will return to their position in society as useful and productive citizens. If this book can help prepare those patients and their families who are in this middle group to handle the mental anguish of open-heart surgery, then I have achieved my goal.

How well a patient does following surgery is dependent upon his attitude prior to entering the operating room. It is extremely difficult to develop the proper attitude following surgery. When I talk to patients pre-operatively to make this point, I frequently use the example of a football team. The days prior to a game must be spent getting the players ready, both physically and mentally, for their opponent. Very few teams can go into the locker room at half time, behind 30–0, and have their coach give a pep talk that results in their coming out and defeating the other team. The patient must realize that it is not always the team with the best players that wins, but rather the team with the greatest *desire*.

As far as I'm concerned, patients should view the day of open-heart surgery as the biggest "game" of their lives and they should go into it with just this attitude. If they can say and think, "you get me through the surgery tomorrow, then I'll do every-

thing you ask me to do; you just do your job, and I'll do the rest,"
I am confident they will do well.

In no way is this book intended to set a standard for other
physicians in the medical and surgical management of open-
heart patients. There are as many approaches to caring for these
patients as there are cardiovascular surgeons and internists; such
diversity leads to excellence. Cardiac surgery is not a static discipline, and I find myself frequently changing techniques as well
as my approach to patients. In the future, I hope to have the
courage to continue to change.

The book that follows is simply a personal approach based on
actual people and cases cared for by me and my team. Our commitment to perfection and excellence in the operating room is
surpassed only by our dedication to the psychological preparation
and emotional support of the patients and their families. Every
effort is made to portray the exact emotions and feelings of each
individual as best as I can recall. The names of the patients have
been changed to protect their identity. The rest is fact.

Fear of the unknown is overwhelming and difficult for anyone to handle under the best of circumstances. Anxiety over what
is expected, especially pertaining to open-heart surgery, is normal
and understandable. Through this book I shall attempt to convey
my approach to the emotional preparation of the patient and the
family so that they might be better prepared to handle a very
difficult situation. I will not try to convince you of the safety of
open-heart surgery, for that has already been stated as a statistical
fact. What I will try to do is give you as much insight as possible
into the risks and complications of coronary artery bypass surgery.
I will try to inform you of what might be expected should you
undergo this operation, as well as what you might expect during
the recovery period.

It is more important to smile and be grateful you're alive than
to focus on post-op pain and discomfort. I hope to help future

patients realize that it really isn't any more painful to smile, and to reassure loved ones than it is to frown and selfishly upset their families. I will not tolerate the latter, and I demand the former. This is clearly established with every patient pre-operatively, when it matters the most, when I say *"Smile . . . or I'll kick your bed!*

Thanks are due to many people who have made this book possible—to my wife, Sylvia, and our fine sons, Monte and Gary, who have been so understanding and supportive during the years of my training and practice; to Julie Manternach, who, as a constant companion, shared with me the joy of success, the agony of decisions, and the heartbreak of losing a patient; to the skilled surgeons who trained me, especially Ronald C. Elkins, M.D., G. Rainey Williams, M.D., and John A. Schilling, M.D.; to the many physicians who have asked me to participate in the care of their patients; and to the patients and their families who have entrusted their lives to me.

I must also thank those who have wholeheartedly given of themselves for me and my patients: the OR personnel, especially Helen Williamson, Pat Eaton, and Laura Acree; the pump team, Bill Fiddler, Ron Lawson, and Rick Booth; the ICU and Eight West nursing staffs; and the remaining nursing staff of St. John's Hospital, as well as the ancillary support personnel who are so vital in providing care.

I could never forget my parents, who, through their love and Christian example, helped me to become sensitive to those in need, yet unafraid to show compassion, despite the risk of loss.

Finally, my appreciation goes to Pam and Jack Garoutte for the encouragement that kept me going, and to Carol Houck Smith and George P. Brockway whose belief in this work made it a reality.

Smile ...
or I'll Kick
Your Bed!

1

THE HOT Sunday afternoon sun dropped below treetop level as we approached the eighteenth tee. The shade from the trees and the gentle breeze were a welcome relief from the stifling heat of the previous seventeen holes we had just completed walking. It seemed as though I had spent much of my time getting out of sand traps during the round.

Sylvia, my wife, looked fresh as always, but her strength had been sapped after carrying her clubs all afternoon. Her tee shot was similar to the last three holes and was somewhat disappointing.

Monte, our older son, who had just turned sixteen, prepared to tee his ball as Gary, our other son, moved to the side. As usual, Monte's tee shot was long, and hooked just the right amount back into the center of the fairway.

Two days earlier, Gary, who was only nine, had shot an unbelievable round of one hundred one for eighteen holes. Now he teed his ball up and also hit an excellent shot that faded somewhat at the last, but was still in the fairway.

As I prepared for my shot, I looked off to the white clubhouse and, just east of this, to the tall buildings of downtown. Suddenly I found it difficult to concentrate on the mechanics of a golf swing. In approximately two hours I would be facing Walter and his family, presenting to them the risks and complications of his open-heart surgery, scheduled for just over twelve hours from now. No matter how hard I tried, I could not keep from thinking about him. At the age of thirty-nine, Walter was only two years older than I was, and he was in need of six or seven bypass grafts. I took a slow, deliberate backswing, then brought the club head through the ball. It mattered little that I had sliced it into the rough. More important things were on my mind than the position of my tee shot.

The events of the past three weeks had been overwhelming for Walter and his family. About six years earlier he had suffered a heart attack and had undergone a heart catheterization soon after that. Blockages in the heart arteries were found, but were not felt to be significant enough to warrant bypass surgery. He had been seen by his physician at frequent intervals and was maintained on medical management with excellent results. He had undergone a treadmill test approximately eighteen months ago, which was interpreted as normal. The recent onset of frequent chest pain brought on by mild to moderate exertion, such as yardwork or climbing stairs, indicated the need for a repeat treadmill. This time the results were markedly positive, and Walter had been admitted for a cardiac catheterization one week ago.

The heart cath had been less frightening for Walter this time; he knew what to expect. Again, he had been securely strapped into a special cradlelike X-ray table. His arms were uncomfortably extended above his head so that they would not hinder the efforts to obtain clear pictures of his heart arteries. The cradle was rotated to the desired position to best expose each coronary vessel. This frequent rotation of the cradle, back and forth, had made Walter feel more like a shish kebab over a fire than a patient.

First, the doctor deadened Walter's right groin. Then, through a small puncture site, he threaded a plastic catheter through the groin artery up to Walter's heart, carefully watching it on the TV screen located above and behind Walter's right shoulder.

The first injection of the dye material was into Walter's left ventricle, or main pumping chamber. Each contraction dispersed the dye throughout the arteries of his body, causing him to experience a hot, flushed feeling all over. This larger catheter was then removed and a smaller catheter was inserted into the right groin artery and advanced to the area of the heart. Again, the procedure was monitored on the TV screen. The small catheter was then manipulated into the orifices of his two main coronary arteries, and multiple movies were made during each injection of dye. The cradle was rotated to a different position for each of the multiple "camera shots" in order to give a different viewing angle of each vessel as it was filled with the dye. The only sounds Walter recalled were the whir of the movie camera, the techs calling out his blood pressure and pulse rate, and—after every injection of dye—the doctor's command, "Cough!" Walter responded with vigorous coughs, unaware that this simple maneuver would cause his heart to speed up, allowing his blood to clear the dye from his coronary arteries.

The cath had revealed significant progression of Walter's coronary artery disease (blockages in the heart arteries), and I had been asked to see him in consultation. I had presented the results of his cath. With the recent change in his symptoms despite medications, one of three things would occur. He would undoubtedly have progression in the frequency and severity of his angina, or heart pain. He could possibly have a mild to moderate heart attack, similar to the one he had suffered six years ago. Or, finally, he might suffer a massive heart attack, which would either cost him his life or make him a cardiac cripple. I could not, and would not, attempt to predict which of the three would occur and when. I also presented to him his choices of treatment. Walter chose surgery, for he felt that it offered him the best chance of returning to a relatively normal life, which included his somewhat pressured job as an accountant.

Because of scheduling problems and because Walter wanted to take care of family affairs, he had been discharged from the hospital, to be readmitted five days later. Surgery was to be the following morning. I strongly advised him to stop smoking, or at least to cut back before surgery in order to reduce the chances of post-op lung complications. I knew that the stress he would experience while waiting for surgery would make it difficult for him to quit.

At about the same time that I was starting my round of golf, Walter was driving to St. John's Hospital. The fear that he might never see his home again was in his mind. The drive to St. John's was made in silence. His wife, Becky, sat beside him, staring out the window and trying to hide her shock that this was really happening. It is not uncommon for families to have feelings of "why is this happening to us?" or "how could you do this to me?" These feelings are based on fear of what lies ahead.

During the admission process Walter could not keep from breaking into a sweat as the lab technician placed a rubber tourniquet around his arm. She drew what seemed to be an excessive amount of blood for admission lab work and type and cross match for transfusions. The other admission tests, such as electrocardiogram, chest X-ray, and routine laboratory studies, were not nearly as traumatic for him as the "vampire ceremony" of drawing blood.

It was disappointing to him that the laboratory personnel and other technicians failed to acknowledge him as a patient admitted for open-heart surgery. Quite understandably, he considered himself a special admission, and it was disheartening that they didn't seem to feel the same way. He had no way of knowing that these people had performed the same procedures on countless other patients earlier that day prior to his admission. They probably had almost as many more to do after him. To them he was just another name and face.

The nurse on the floor to which Walter was assigned asked the usual questions about previous hospitalizations, allergies, and medications. He was weighed, and vital signs (blood pressure, temperature, pulse, and respiratory rate) were taken. He then settled back to a quiet but apprehensive afternoon until I would arrive at the prearranged time of 8:00 P.M. Conversation initiated by Becky was sporadic and evasive, touching on the weather, the news, or various articles in the morning paper. She was desperately trying to keep him from thinking about their two young children, whom he had kissed good-by possibly for the last time, and about what would happen during the next twenty-four hours.

It is sad how patients and their families are so unable to deal with significant illness or potential death. Generally they attempt to avoid the subjects by discussing inconsequential topics in an uncomfortable effort to divert their thoughts from painful possibilities. How much better it would be if they would openly discuss their apprehensions, hopes, and feelings of fear. Too often they falsely believe that they are protecting one another by not engaging in such discussions. We all need to recognize this, and to encourage an open exchange between patients and their loved ones.

As Walter lit a cigarette and tried to concentrate on a novel, he was distracted by feelings of hostility and anger. Many people he knew and worked with imbibed greater quantities of alcohol, smoked more, and lived a much looser life than he did. Yet none of them had suffered a heart attack nor was anyone else about to undergo open-heart surgery.

Another laboratory technician arrived to draw arterial blood gases from the artery in his wrist. This test would measure the amount of oxygen that his blood had picked up from his lungs.

It was much more painful than his other blood-letting experiences, as it was drawn directly from an artery instead of a vein.

After the technician had drawn the blood, a nurse entered with a small yellow plastic bottle containing an antiseptic soap solution. She instructed Walter to take a shower now and later in the evening. He was to wash with the special soap from chin to toes, especially concentrating on the breastbone area and legs.

After a long shower, Walter got back into bed, lit a cigarette, and began again to read the novel. Within a few minutes his mind was flooded with questions and apprehension. Meanwhile, Becky tried vainly to keep him from thinking of the very things that neither could avoid.

2

AFTER a shower and a sandwich, I quickly changed from golfer to physician. The drive to St. John's seemed much shorter than it actually was. Deep in thought, I had only vague recall of the stop lights, turns on and off the freeway, or the other cars I met or passed. I was amazed to find myself suddenly driving into the parking lot of my office building, located just across the street from St. John's.

Julie, my surgical assistant and a cardiovascular clinical specialist, had become an integral part of the team in the pre-op preparation of the patients. She was early, as usual, and during the wait she concentrated on her role in helping this patient and his family better understand and cope with the information to be presented. Later, while showing the family the Waiting Room and the Intensive Care Unit, she would use the observations she had made during the pre-op talk as a means of reinforcing all that I had discussed with them.

Before going to the tenth floor, where Walter and his family were waiting, Julie and I reviewed Walter's heart catheterization films. These showed good left ventricular pumping function, but severe, diffuse (scattered) blockages in all major coronary arteries and their primary branches. This was the fourth or fifth time we had looked at these films. I felt that at least six—and possibly seven—bypass grafts would be required. We were humbled by, and apprehensive about, the procedure to be performed in the morning.

As the elevator door closed and began its ascent, I had to decide whether or not to present all the risks and possible complications to Walter and his family. This decision came up with almost every pre-op talk because I knew that what I had to say would be extremely upsetting. It would be much easier—and quicker—to walk in, introduce myself, reassure Walter that he would do well tomorrow, and walk out.

But I could never do things that way. First, I must deal with patients and their families with honesty and openness. Second, I must establish a rapport pre-operatively with those entrusted to my care. And finally, I must come to know my patients and their families so well that I will be able to empathize with them in times of sorrow as well as rejoice with them in times of joy.

On numerous occasions I have been warned by fellow physicians that I was getting "too close" to my patients and their families, thereby setting myself up for potentially devastating emotional traumas. But I had turned away from this advice in favor of the creed of ABC's *Wide World of Sports*—"the thrill of victory and the agony of defeat." For I feel that if I avoid getting close to patients because of the threat of the "agony of defeat," I will never be close enough to experience with them the "thrill of victory." More important, I believe that the greatest test of one's spirit is to listen to one's own heart when other people are saying something different.

I will never forget one summer night during the final year of my residency. A young boy in his late teens had been brought to the Emergency Room in extremely critical condition. He had suffered a gunshot wound to the lower chest and upper abdomen. I immediately rushed him to surgery in an attempt to save his life. The next seven hours were horrible! The struggle to save the boy's life began to slip from my grasp, and I finally had to succumb to defeat, despite transfusing over thirty units of blood.

Tired and depressed, I left the OR to console the victim's family, whom I had never met. I had no way of knowing that not a single message that I had sent from the OR had ever reached the family. Each message had progressively portrayed a more pessimistic prognosis. The boy's parents had been at a party, and for the initial six hours after their son's injury they had been unaware of my efforts to save his life. Only in the last hour had the eighteen family members and close friends begun to assemble in the hospital lobby.

"Are you the family of the boy who was shot?" I asked in a subdued tone. I didn't even know the boy's name. He had no identification when seen in the Emergency Room.

"My son's going to be all right, isn't he?" the boy's mother implored, as she rose quickly from the couch in the lobby.

I walked to her and took her hands in mine. "Didn't you get the messages I sent during surgery?" I didn't have to ask, for I could see that the family was totally unprepared for what I had to tell them. "Ma'am, your son expired in surgery just a few minutes ago. I am the chief resident who performed the surgery. I did everything I possibly could."

What ensued was one of the most horrifying experiences of my career. The mother became hysterical. She abused me physically by slapping and hitting at me. But the verbal attack from the entire family was even more painful. They accused me of being personally responsible for the boy's death, despite my attempts to explain that his was a fatal injury from the onset. What made it even worse, these people were strangers.

I made a solemn promise to myself that I would never again talk with a family following surgery without having made every effort possible to meet them pre-operatively. I would then be able to look them squarely in the eye, call each by first name, and say, "I did the best I could," knowing that they would believe me.

The elevator door opened, and I emerged with renewed determination to proceed with the pre-op talk. No matter how upsetting it would be to Walter and his family, the only way I could establish the relationship I sought was to have them realistically acknowledge the potential risks of surgery, including death.

3

I KNOCKED gently on the door and peered into the room to be sure everyone was presentable.

"Hi, Doc," Walter blurted out, obviously relieved to see me. He extinguished his cigarette, somewhat embarrassed that I had caught him smoking.

Walter and I had first met five days earlier when I had explained to him the findings of his heart catheterization and had recommended that he have surgery. That meeting had been cordial and friendly, but certainly had not been one that could be described as developing a close bond between us. Now, Walter knew that we were meeting for the sole purpose of preparing Becky and him for surgery scheduled tomorrow morning.

"Becky, are there other family members coming?" I asked. I always wanted those who would be waiting during surgery to be present for the pre-op talk. Walter informed me that both of his parents had died years ago from heart attack. Becky's parents lived in Iowa and would not be coming for the surgery. Becky and Walter's children were too young to understand the pre-op talk. They would be spending the next several days with friends.

After I had introduced Julie, I turned to Walter. "I'll go over the findings of your heart cath once again." On my prescription pad I drew a picture of Walter's heart and the aorta (the large

artery that comes out of the heart), as well as his coronary arteries. In addition, I sketched in the arteries leading to his brain,
arms and legs. These were drawn upside down from my position,
but right side up for Walter and Becky. I had become quite adept
at this, and although my drawing was not a work of art, it served
its purpose.

Having completed the drawing of the heart, aorta, and coronary arteries, I said, "This is what your heart and its coronary
arteries looked like when you were twenty years old" (see Figure
1, page 26). I checked to see if Walter and Becky were following
what I had presented, then began to draw in each individual
blockage. "This is what your heart looks like now." As I completed my drawing, it became apparent that seven primary
branches of Walter's three main coronary arteries were involved
with significant blockages (see Figure 2, page 27). I paused to
give Walter and Becky a chance to comprehend the significance
of what I had just drawn.

"There are three alternatives to choose from in this situation.
First, you can go home and do nothing, letting nature take its
course. Second, you can continue on medications, which will
offer some relief of your angina. The problem with medications
is that they do not clean out the coronary arteries or change the
blockage situation. They only alleviate the chest pain that you
have been having. The third alternative is open-heart surgery,
where we take the vein out of your leg and use it to bypass each
of these blockages."

At this point I carefully drew in the vein bypass grafts and
showed how three separate vein segments would be used to bypass the seven different blockages. One vein segment would bypass three of the blocked arteries, and each of the other two segments of vein would bypass two blocked arteries (see Figure 3,
page 28).

Walter and Becky looked at me in disbelief. The fact that I

was going to use only three vein segments to bypass seven arteries needed further clarification.

"I can see from your expressions that you don't completely understand what I have just presented. The end of the vein will go into the side of one heart artery. As the vein passes over another blocked artery, a hole cut in the side of the vein will be sewn to a hole cut in the side of the artery. As it passes over a third artery, another hole will be cut in the side of the vein and will be sewn to a hole cut in the side of the artery. The same procedure will be repeated with the other two segments of vein, with each one of them being attached to only two heart arteries instead of three. The other end of each vein segment will then be sutured to separate holes cut into the aorta, the large artery coming out of your heart. This will provide the source of blood supply for each of the vein bypass grafts."

"How much greater is the risk of doing seven bypasses instead of three?" Becky asked.

"That's a good question. The risk is not significantly greater to bypass seven heart arteries than four or five. A much greater risk exists if I only bypass three, when five, six, or seven could have been bypassed. Any blocked heart arteries of significant size that are left unbypassed only lead to further problems with angina. The reason we do the operation is to relieve this problem."

I now put the difficult question to Walter. "I assume, since you're here, that you've decided that surgery is your choice of treatment. Is that correct?"

"After looking at those drawings I don't think I have any other choice," Walter said in a somewhat resigned manner. Nervously he lit another cigarette. I was aware of his heavy smoking habit, but felt that this was not the time to discuss this issue.

"Becky," I said, "do you understand what we are talking about? Are you agreeable?"

She nodded her approval, but with reluctance. "This is

Figure 1 • WALTER'S HEART BEFORE

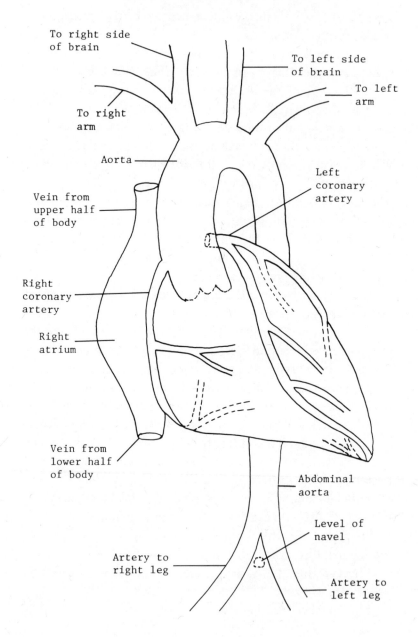

To right side
of brain

To left side
of brain

To left
arm

To right
arm

Aorta

Left
coronary
artery

Vein from
upper half
of body

Right
coronary
artery

Right
atrium

Vein from
lower half
of body

Abdominal
aorta

Level of
navel

Artery to
right leg

Artery to
left leg

Figure 2 • WALTER'S HEART NOW

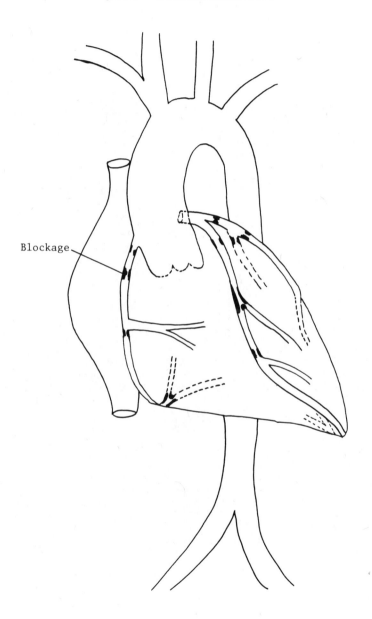

Blockage

Figure 3 · Vein Bypass Grafts in Place

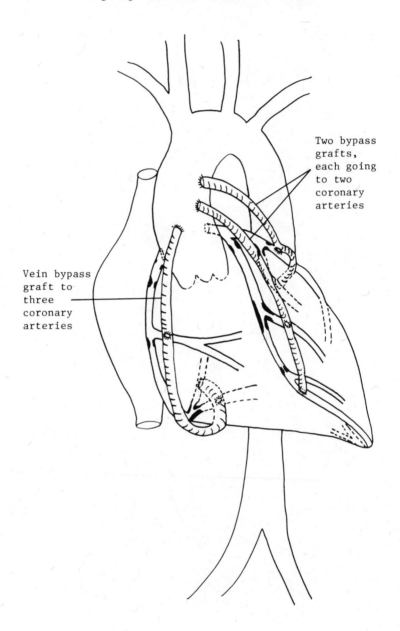

Two bypass
grafts,
each going
to two
coronary
arteries

Vein bypass
graft to
three
coronary
arteries

something that Walter has got to decide."

"I totally agree, and I feel strongly that this should always be the case." I looked at Walter. "It's not fair, or right, for Becky to make this decision. If she did, she would carry the burden of guilt for the rest of her life if tomorrow doesn't turn out as we all hope it will. You must make this decision yourself."

"As I see it, I have no other choice." This time there was more acceptance in his voice.

I moved my chair back so that Becky and Walter were directly in front of me, and then embarked on the most painful and difficult part of the pre-op talk. This is the portion that I had contemplated omitting completely. But in the past I had always gone ahead with the entire pre-op talk for every patient and family. Almost without exception they had commented after surgery on how much the talk had helped to prepare them for the events of the next day.

"Well, then, if you're agreeable, I need to talk to you about the risks involved. Walter, the risk of your operation is in the range of five percent. This means that you still have a ninety-five-percent chance that you will come through the surgery tomorrow and do fine. There is an eighty to ninety percent chance that most, if not all, of your angina will be relieved. But percentages are just numbers. They give you some idea of what you're up against. If you make it, you will not care what my results are with the next one hundred open-heart patients; and if you don't make it, your family won't be impressed that you were the only patient that I lost out of those next hundred cases. What you must realize is that if things don't go exactly the way I plan, then it could be all over tomorrow.

"You now have what I call the 'Redd Foxx Syndrome.' " With that, I clutched my chest with one hand, raised the other hand in the air and went through the "Sanford and Son" routine of "Oh, oh! This is the biggie! This is the biggie!"

Everyone laughed, but I quickly added, "That may be funny on TV, but it isn't funny at all if it is *your* heart." The laughter subsided. "Now that you know what your heart arteries look like, every time you have chest pain you are going to wonder 'Is this the biggie?' or will it go away like the last episode of pain did with nitroglycerin? During the past five days, while you were at home, I'll bet you and Becky went through the 'Redd Foxx Syndrome.' Knowing how bad your heart arteries are, she is almost afraid to leave you alone. If she does leave, she's afraid of what she might find when she returns. I'm sure that during the night she has instinctively reached over to feel if you're still breathing.

Becky and Walter nodded. They had indeed experienced what I had described.

"The risk of surgery is based on three main things. If the overall risk is five percent, then by far the greatest percentage can be attributed to the risk of having a heart attack during the operation. The heart arteries that I have drawn on this sheet of paper," I gestured toward the drawing that I had laid on the foot of the bed, "are not nearly as large as I have drawn them. They are approximately the size of the end of my ball point pen." I drew a Papermate pen out of my pocket, and punched the button, extruding the small point. "This point is about two millimeters in diameter. A coronary artery that is this size is a large one. Most of your arteries are even smaller."

Hearing this, Becky uncomfortably shifted position. Walter lit another cigarette. I continued, "There is no way that Becky could darn my sock if my foot kept moving." I illustrated this by crossing my legs, moving my foot in a kicking type motion. "By the same token, Walter, there is no way that I can work on your tiny coronary arteries with your heart beating. Therefore we must stop your heart!" A concerned expression appeared on the faces of my attentive audience.

"I stop your heart by placing a clamp across the aorta, the

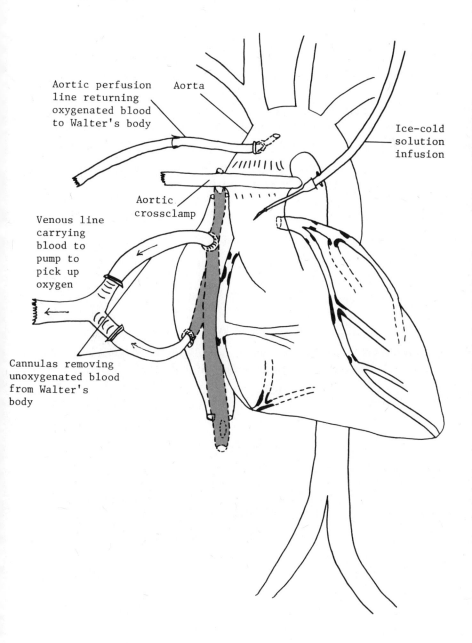

Figure 4 • ON THE PUMP WITH WALTER'S HEART STOPPED

Aortic perfusion line returning oxygenated blood to Walter's body

Aorta

Ice-cold solution infusion

Aortic crossclamp

Venous line carrying blood to pump to pick up oxygen

Cannulas removing unoxygenated blood from Walter's body

large blood vessel coming out of your heart. The heart-lung machine will take over the function of your heart and pump blood to your brain, kidneys, liver, intestines, and other vital organs. But the clamp will be between the line from the heart-lung machine and your heart, thus cutting off the blood supply to the heart arteries. This causes the heart to stop. If you think about it for a minute, a heart attack occurs when one small artery is blocked off. With the clamp across the aorta, it will completely block off the blood supply to all of the heart arteries [see Figure 4, page 31]. Therefore, the greatest risk of the surgery is the possibility of a heart attack. As recently as ten years ago, the death rate with this type of operation could have been as high as fifteen to twenty percent. The risk today, in your case, is exactly as I have explained it to you. The reason for the improved outlook is the development of new methods for protecting the heart during the time that it is without its blood supply. We protect your heart, first, by cooling your body to around eighty degrees, and then by cooling your heart to approximately forty degrees. You have undoubtedly heard that if one of your fingers is severed, you should pack it in ice and bring it to the hospital. The reason for this is that the ice decreases the need for oxygen by the tissue, which is without blood supply. We use the same principle to protect your heart.

"Despite everything that we might do to try to protect your heart, there is still the danger of a heart attack. It is most likely to occur during the time when your heart is stopped, without blood supply so that we can sew the vein bypass grafts into your coronary arteries. There is also a risk of heart attack while we put you to sleep, or as we try to get you on the heart-lung machine. But, by far, the greatest risk occurs while your heart is without its blood supply.

"The second risk is obvious. We are going to be cutting holes in your aorta and heart to put you on the heart-lung machine, as well as cutting small holes in the coronary arteries and sewing in multiple bypass grafts. Therefore, there is the possibility of hemorrhage.

"I'm not concerned about hemorrhage during the operation. As long as Julie and I are standing right there, we should be able to control almost any bleeding that might occur. I am more concerned about the first two or three hours post-op, when we have you back in the ICU. Suddenly, because of the constant pressure from the pulsation of blood, something pulls loose. We now have a massive hemorrhage situation where you fill a quart bottle in ten seconds. If that should occur, because your chest is closed, we will need to rush you back to the OR.

"The risk of hemorrhage is probably less than one-half percent of the total five percent. If it doesn't happen within the first few hours post-op, it is unusual for it to occur anytime after that. It is not something you need to worry about six weeks, or even two days after surgery.

"The third risk is the one I really hate to talk about. It will probably be the most upsetting to you, and certainly is the most upsetting to me as your surgeon." I pointed to the plastic tube on my drawing that carries blood back to the body from the heart-lung machine. "This tube enters just below the blood vessels to the brain and the arms" (see Figure 4). "One small air bubble, one piece of hardening of the artery that's knocked off as I push this plastic tube into the aorta, or one small clot that is pumped back to the body from the heart-lung machine can cause problems. If it goes to the arteries of the feet or hands there is the risk of gangrene. If it goes to the kidneys, it can cause kidney failure. These are serious complications, but they are treatable and usually are not life-threatening. But if a clot or air bubble goes up one of the arteries to the brain, it causes a stroke. If it's a small air bubble or clot, you will have a minor stroke. If it's a large air bubble or clot, the result could be anything from permanent paralysis to never waking up after surgery."

Attempting to reassure Walter and Becky, I quickly went on.

"Don't focus on stroke. I am much more worried about heart attack than I am about stroke. I just want you to be aware that this can happen. If it's a small stroke and you work with me, the chances are that you'll regain most, if not all, of the function of the paralyzed parts. If it's a massive stroke, you will never wake up. Again, if you can, don't focus on stroke. The chance of this happening is in the range of less than one-half percent of the total five percent. It's just the risk I hate the most because it is so disheartening to me to have you come off the pump without having a heart attack, have no problems with bleeding, and then have you never regain consciousness after surgery. That is the most difficult type of case for me to handle, and I feel it's only fair that you and Becky know about it beforehand.

"The other complications associated with surgery are more obvious. When incisions are made from the top of your breastbone almost to your navel, and from your groin to ankle to remove the vein, there is the danger of infection. That's the reason we've had you wash with the special soap and will put you on antibiotics before surgery. Even with these precautions, infection may occur. If it is superficial, it is not usually a problem. But if it is a deep infection, involving the sternum, or breastbone, then the healing process is long and sometimes complicated.

"Another problem is pneumonia. Once you've had your chest split down the middle, it is hard to cough and to take deep breaths. You'll feel as though a safe was dropped out of this tenth-story window and landed on your chest. Or, you will feel as though Becky backed the car over your chest and left it there while she got out to see what you were yelling about.

"Because you are such a heavy smoker, you are more susceptible to pneumonia. Therefore, in your case, it will be much more important for you to cough. Because of the pain, it will be extremely difficult for you to take deep breaths, much less cough. But you must cough! I'll be damned if we'll go through six or seven hours of surgery, then have you die a week later of pneumonia, when it could have been prevented. You will cough! I will make you cough! You will learn to hate every cigarette that you have ever smoked, but we won't have problems with pneumonia! Is that clear?"

Walter nodded in agreement and immediately crushed out the cigarette he had lit a few minutes ago.

I now turned to Becky. "Walter has it easy tomorrow. If he does well, he won't be aware of this for six to eight hours after surgery. If he doesn't make it, he won't know the difference. As far as I'm concerned, Becky, *you* have it tough tomorrow. Sitting downstairs for six or seven hours will be a lonesome and horrible experience. I will do everything I can to make it as easy on you as possible—by keeping you informed with the truth. From what we have discussed so far, you can see that I'll shoot pretty straight with you. No matter how things are going in surgery, I will let you know, good or bad."

During my residency I sat with a fraternity brother and his family while his father underwent open-heart surgery. Each question that I was able to answer prompted more questions and deeper discussion. It soon became apparent that the family had been told very little about the surgical procedure and its associated risks. The family members' uninformed state was even more unsettling to me when, as the day progressed, I realized that they were not being given any information from the OR about the progress of surgery. Finally, after five and one-half hours of increasing anxiety and tension, I made an attempt to find out how the patient was doing. It was only then that I learned that he was doing well and had been in the ICU for almost an hour.

This episode, along with the traumatic experience of the boy with the gunshot wound, had solidified my determination to keep families well informed throughout the surgical procedure. And so my "multiple phone calls to family" routine evolved. Admittedly, pre-operatively, I give the families an expanded time frame, allowing for unforeseen crises that might arise during surgery. The primary reason for the calls is to make the wait for families as tolerable as possible. The phone calls also serve to keep families informed of complications, thereby laying the groundwork for potentially devastating news. I will never again walk into a surgical waiting room after surgery to face a family that has not been forewarned and prepared for bad news.

"Becky, this is the plan for tomorrow. Surgery is scheduled for seven forty A.M. Walter will get his 'Whoopee Shot' [hypo] about six forty and will leave for the Operating Room shortly thereafter. I suggest you see him before he's had his 'Whoopee Shot,' because after that he won't care whether you're there or not. So, you should be at the hospital about six.

"When he leaves for surgery, go with him on the elevator to the third floor. He will go to the Holding Room, and you should go to the Waiting Room, which is located on the same floor. Julie will take you down later this evening to familiarize you with the ICU and show you where you should wait. The surgery time of seven forty A.M. is the time that we will move Walter into the Operating Room, not the time surgery will actually start. Once he is in the OR, it will take approximately thirty to forty-five minutes to start the i.v.'s, put him to sleep, and put in the rest of the tubes. I will explain these tubes to you later. When he is asleep and all of the tubes and lines are in, I will call to let you know how things are going. I will tell you if he is doing well, if his blood pressure has dropped, if his heart has speeded up, or if we've had any other problems.

"Of course, I hope I'll be able to call and tell you things are fine.

"It will then take Julie and me twenty minutes to wash our hands, prep Walter from chin to toes, drape him, and finally start the operation. Therefore, if I call you at eight fifteen, it will be about eight thirty-five before we make the first skin incision.

"At this point many people ask: Who assists me during the operation? You're looking at her—Julie is my assistant. There are a lot of other people in the room helping us, but we do the surgery. We first take the vein from the leg. We feel very strongly that preparing the vein is one of the most critical parts of the operation. Great care is taken in dissecting it out.

"It takes roughly an hour to remove the vein. Once we have it out, we'll move up and make the chest incision. It then takes around an hour to get on the heart-lung machine, or the pump. We call it the pump because it takes over the pumping function of the heart. Because this is such an important step, I will have a nurse call you when we are on the pump. She will let you know that we are on the pump and doing okay or that we have had some technical problems getting on the pump, but are all right now. But if the message is that we had to 'crash' on the pump, that means that Walter suddenly had a heart attack and we had to go on the pump rapidly. If this is the message, the risk of the operation has increased substantially. But if things go as expected, we will be able to tell you that we are on the pump and Walter's okay.

"After going on the pump, we stop the heart and then start sewing in the bypass grafts. It takes about twenty-five to thirty minutes per bypass. Since we are planning on doing seven bypasses, we are talking about almost three hours on the pump. It probably will not be quite that long—this is only an approximation. Once we get the seven bypasses sutured to the heart arteries, we will be able to remove the clamp from the aorta. This will reestablish blood flow to the heart, allowing it to start beating again. Therefore, the heart will be without blood supply only while we have it stopped to sew in the coronary artery portion of the bypass grafts. When this has been completed, we will call and let you know that we are halfway through the bypass procedure and we can only tell you we are doing satisfactorily. The mere fact that Walter's heart starts to beat again tells us nothing about how well it will function on its own. We have no way of knowing how well we have protected the heart while it was without its vital blood supply. Only later, when we try to come off the heart-lung machine, will we learn if Walter has suffered a heart attack or not. If he hasn't, then his heart will be able to take over its normal pumping functions.

"Then comes the most important phone call of all. It will be: 'We're off the pump and we're doing fine. We're off the pump, we've had some problems, but we're doing all right now. Or, we're having difficulty getting him off the heart-lung machine, and we're in big trouble.' That means just that. We would no longer be talking about a risk of five percent; we're talking about a risk of ninety-five percent. There are a lot of things we can do with drugs and other special equipment, which I won't explain at this time, but if we have to resort to these, we're in real danger of losing him."

Noting Becky's apprehension, I tried to calm her. "We all hope that the message won't be the third one. I will send the message that we're off the heart-lung machine and we're doing fine only if Walter comes off the pump the first time. Usually this is not the case, especially when the heart is without blood flow as long as Walter's will be. His heart is bound to be somewhat sluggish for the first hour or so after the pump run. Therefore, we are usually required to use one or more drugs to stimulate the heart to help it come off the pump. It is not unusual to have to use these drugs, and you should not be alarmed if we send the message, 'We're off the heart-lung machine, we've had some problems, but we're doing okay now.' I fully expect this to be the message in Walter's case.

"The last phone call from surgery will be made to let you know that we are closing. The nurse will make this call when we are sure that all of the sites where we have cut into the heart to put Walter on the pump and all of the suture lines of the bypass grafts are secure. This should occur roughly thirty to forty minutes after we come off the pump. Of all the times I have given you, the time it takes to close the chest and to move Walter from surgery to the Intensive Care Unit is fixed at one hour and fifteen minutes. All of the other times have been approximations, but this is a very definite time. Once we get him to the ICU and are sure he is stable, Julie and I will come to the Waiting Room to talk to you. We'll take you to see him, and we will go in with you that first time.

"You need to be prepared for how terrible Walter will look when you first see him. He will have gained between ten to fifteen pounds from the fluid that is pumped in from the heart-lung machine. Much of this will be in his face, especially around the mouth and eyelids. He will look extremely puffy. In addition, he will be very pale because the tremendous amount of fluid will dilute his color. He will also be painted from chin to toes with an antiseptic solution. Finally, he may be shivering because he will still be a little cold. Even though he looks terrible, if I say he's doing okay, you must believe me.

"In addition, there will be multiple tubes, i.v. lines, and perhaps blood transfusions. There will be a TV screen above the head of the bed that has his electrocardiogram and arterial pressure pattern on it. There will also be a large blue breathing machine at his bedside. In short, he will look much like the Six Million Dollar Man. He will not look like what you might expect from watching television, where open-heart patients are often portrayed sitting up and eating lunch minutes after surgery."

Even though I had not been looking at Walter directly, I was aware that he had been shifting position frequently and had glanced out the window several times. He was trying to appear as unaffected as possible, almost dissociating himself from what was being said. Walter's eyes now met mine and held for a second. I knew that what came next would get his attention.

"In addition to looking horrible, it will be very frightening for you, Walter, if you don't know what to expect when you begin to come out of the anesthetic. You will have a tube the size of my index finger that will go through your nose or mouth into your windpipe. It will not go into your stomach, but into the windpipe through the voicebox. The tube will be connected to a breathing machine. This tube is made of hard plastic and will be extremely uncomfortable. In fact, it will just plain hurt. Many patients complain after surgery that this tube was the worst part. You'll be tempted to pull it out, but don't! That is my tube and you leave it alone! I will take it out when you show me that you can breathe well on your own. Since the tube passes between your vocal cords, you will be unable to talk. The nurses are very good at interpreting your needs. Just point or gesture if you need something for pain or anything else. They will be able to figure out what you need.

"You'll also have an i.v. that goes into the side of your neck or under your collar bone. This i.v. line goes down into the right atrium, or filling chamber, to measure the volume of blood returning to your heart. It is called a central venous pressure line, or CVP.

"You will have two i.v.'s in the left arm for fluids or transfusions and you'll have an i.v. in the artery in your right wrist. This line in your artery is connected to a pressure monitor that will continually measure your blood pressure during the entire operation and in the ICU post-op.

"You will have two chest tubes that are as big around as my thumb that go through the upper part of your abdomen, under the breast bone to drain out the bleeding from around your heart. Some bleeding is normal. I'm not worried about oozing that might occur. That is expected. When I talk about hemorrhage,

I'm talking about filling up a gallon jug in thirty seconds. As long as the blood is merely oozing, I will not be concerned.

"Finally, you will have a small catheter that will pass through your penis into your bladder to measure kidney output while you're on the heart-lung machine and during the post-op period. This catheter has a balloon on the end of it to keep it in place. Your bladder will go into spasm around the balloon and give you the sensation that you need to pee. Go ahead and pee. You won't wet the bed. It will go out a tube to a collecting bag at the end of the bed."

Walter laughed. "I know what you're talking about. They put one of those things in me when I had my heart attack."

"The two i.v.'s in your left arm and the i.v. in the artery in your right arm will be put in before you go to sleep. All of the other tubes will be put in after you are asleep or at the end of the operation. It hurts like hell to have the i.v. started in the artery in your wrist. I will deaden it the best I can, but it is still painful. This i.v. in your artery will constantly monitor your blood pressure. As I said earlier, one of the most critical times is when we are putting you to sleep. Heart attacks often occur at this time because the blood pressure drops unnoticed. If your pressure drops with the start of anesthesia, we need to know this immediately so we can give you medications to bring it back up. For that reason, we have to start the i.v. in your wrist artery before you are put to sleep."

Relieved, I settled back in my chair. The most difficult part of the pre-op talk was now behind me. "That's enough of the bad stuff. Are you ready for something good?"

Walter and Becky nodded, anxiously anticipating what I would tell them next. I studied Becky's eye's and noted that they were somewhat glassy and tear-filled. For the first time, she seemed to be comprehending all that her husband was up against.

"Walter, my feeling is that your heart will be better tomorrow as soon as we finish the operation than it is right now. All of the blocked arteries will be bypassed, and a new blood supply will be flowing to your heart muscle. There is no other operation like this one that makes a person better immediately. All other operations make people sicker initially. So, if you are better, there is no reason for you to lie around in bed.

"If your vital signs are stable and you show me that you can breathe well on your own, I will pull the tube out of your windpipe within four to six hours after the operation. If you continue to maintain a stable blood pressure, we'll stand you up beside the bed shortly after having the tube removed from your windpipe. You will get up three or four more times during the night. Obviously this will be done only if you're doing well.

"The morning after surgery, which will be Tuesday, most of the tubes and lines, with the possible exception of the chest tubes, will be removed. We will then walk you the length of the ICU. If you continue to progress, we will transfer you sometime Tuesday morning to the postsurgical unit on Eight-West.

"How well you do from that time on will be completely up to you. I have had a few patients home in five days, and even had one man go back to work part time on the seventh day following open-heart surgery."

After what Walter and Becky had heard during the previous forty minutes, they were totally unprepared for this good news. Their surprise was evident, but I was still troubled by Walter's attitude. He had said very little during the entire talk. He had not asked questions, and had worked hard to hide his emotions. I decided to let this ride for the moment and continued. "I have not wanted to terrify or upset you. But I know that many of the things that I have discussed cannot help but do just that. I have gone into such detail for a good reason. Fear of the unknown is overwhelming. Apprehension over an event this serious is normal and expected. I have tried to change the unknowns of open-heart surgery to something that you can comprehend and handle.

"People go into any kind of surgery, but especially open-heart surgery, with two main fears: they have a fear of death and a fear of pain. In addition, after what we have discussed this evening, you must also have a fear of stroke.

"About pain. Pain doesn't bother me a bit. First of all, it's not *my* chest that hurts, it's yours." I said this in a lighthearted manner, then added, "But, seriously, I *want* you to *hurt* tomorrow! You won't experience discomfort during the operation because you'll be asleep. But afterward I want you to have pain from the top of your head to the tip of your toes. Everytime you do, just be grateful you are here to feel it. You realize that the patient who dies and is at the local funeral home tomorrow afternoon, or the patient who has a massive stroke and doesn't ever regain consciousness, never gets the chance to experience post-op pain. Just be grateful that the Lord saw fit to bring you through this operation, and everytime you have pain, give thanks that you're still here to have it. Do you understand what I'm saying?"

There was a new glimmer in Walter's eyes, but it still wasn't the sign of confidence that I needed to see. The next portion of my discussion would address this issue.

"Walter, tomorrow is the biggest 'game' of your life—how well you do depends a great deal on you. Quite frankly, I'm concerned about your attitude going into this operation. I can assure you that if you have the feeling that you won't come out of the OR alive tomorrow, you won't! If you believe that you'll never leave St. John's Hospital alive, let me know right now and you can find someone else to do your surgery. I don't look forward to facing Becky and telling her that you didn't make it. A positive attitude on your part before surgery is the key to success. I feel confident that we can get you through the surgery, but I have to be realistic and recognize that there is a possibility we might not.

There is no question in my mind that some of my patients are alive today only because they had a tremendous desire to live going into the Operating Room."

With the fight in his eyes that I had been waiting for, Walter responded, "If I didn't think I would make it, I damn sure wouldn't have come back to this hospital."

"Okay," I said. "An attitude of 'if I didn't think I would make it' just isn't good enough. I want an attitude that says, 'I'm *going* to make it!'"

Walter sat straight up in bed. "I'm going to make it tomorrow, and I'll do okay!" he said emphatically.

Julie, sitting quietly to my left, had made mental notes of Walter and Becky's every movement and reaction, spoken and unspoken. She could sense my relief when Walter finally began to show the spirit that was so necessary.

I continued, "Now that we have covered the plans for tomorrow, I need to explain two rules that I have. First, I go by Tex, and I expect you to call me that. Don't call me Doctor or Doc! I put my pants on one leg at a time just like you do. You and I will become very close over the next seven to ten days, and when you leave the hospital, I want you to leave as a friend of mine, not just someone I operated on. You don't call your best friend Mister. You call him by his first name. I expect the same. The second rule I have is that you will *smile* whenever Becky, the nurses, Julie, or anyone else enters your room. If you don't, I'll kick your bed! That might not hurt tonight, but I guarantee that it will get your attention tomorrow."

Walter and Becky laughed.

After pausing, I proceeded in a more serious tone. "I will not tolerate you moaning and groaning about how much you hurt, trying to get sympathy from Becky and others. Your family and friends are going to be terrified just seeing you; they will not know how to react or what to say. A smile from you will be very reassuring to them. No matter how much you hurt, I expect you to smile. It doesn't hurt any more to smile than to groan."

By this time, an obvious change had come over Walter and Becky. Their anxiety and fear had now been replaced with an attitude of confidence and calm acceptance. Julie and I could sense this change. We had been through this pre-op talk so many times before that we instinctively knew when it had accomplished its purpose.

I got up, walked over to the bed, and gripped Walter's right hand. There was much more meaning in this handshake than in the initial greeting earlier. With my right hand gripping Walter's and my left hand on his shoulder, our eyes met. Much more was implied than could ever be put into words. "I'll see you in the morning, Walter."

I now turned toward Becky. "I don't shake hands with the ladies, I always hug them." I put my arms around her, placed my cheek next to hers, and whispered in her ear, "We'll take good care of him, and, if God's willing, we'll give him back to you tomorrow."

She nodded, not daring to speak, fearing her voice would betray her emotions.

Julie was now at Walter's side and took his hands in hers. Her dark brown eyes looked into his as she said in her characteristically gentle voice, "Things will go well tomorrow." Later, Walter would say, "From that moment on, I had no doubt that everything would work out all right."

Julie offered to take Becky down to the third floor to show her the Waiting Room and the ICU. Before they left, I said to her, "We ought to be getting Walter settled in the ICU about midafternoon. I will take you in that first time and then you may come back and see Walter again at the regular visiting periods of five thirty and seven thirty tomorrow evening. If everything is going well when you see him at seven thirty, I want you to go home and get some rest. Tomorrow will totally exhaust you, and there is no reason for you to sit around the hospital looking at the walls all night if he's okay. If he's in trouble, we will be here and you're welcome to stay too.

"If you're at home, I'll call you between nine and ten tomorrow night just to let you know how he is. I'll call anytime if there are problems or significant changes in his condition. Here is my card with my home phone number. If you have questions, or if you suddenly awaken during the night and have a strange feeling that something is wrong with Walter, you call me. Don't pace the floor and worry the rest of the night. There's no reason for me to be home asleep when you're awake and upset because you have a feeling that something's wrong."

Becky took the card and gave me her home phone number. As I jotted it down, I intentionally dropped both the Papermate and my black book and said, "That's about the way I am in surgery."

Breaking into a grin, I stooped to pick up the book and pen. Becky and Walter, realizing that my joke was meant to ease the tension, began to laugh. However, I will never forget the time I had done this and the family had taken me seriously. Their horrified expressions had made me realize that this maneuver had to be handled with care.

"Are there any questions?" I studied Becky and Walter, giving them another chance to seek clarification. More important, I was searching for any signs of lack of total commitment to going ahead with surgery. Becky appeared relieved that the pre-op talk was finally over, and all that remained now was the deed itself. Walter seemed to possess an inner strength that had not been present earlier. His positive attitude was reflected by his statement, "I'm ready to go right now."

"That's the spirit. See you in the morning, Walter."

I went to the nurses' station to write the pre-op progress note and orders, while Becky and Julie went to the third floor. During the brief tour of the areas where Becky would spend some very long hours, she revealed to Julie how much she appreciated the time spent explaining in such detail what was to be expected. She felt prepared for what lay ahead and was confident she would never have to doubt Walter's true condition. Knowing that she could call if she became worried or alarmed about any changes she might detect in Walter was comforting. Julie assured her that I was sincere in all that I had said, and encouraged her to call me at any time, even at home.

With the room empty and quiet, Walter got out of bed, picked up the small yellow bottle of surgical soap, and headed for his second shower. He looked forward to its warmth and relaxation. He later told me that it was at this time that he challenged himself to be the best patient that I had ever had.

4

AS I headed home, I reflected upon the pre-op talk with Walter and Becky. I tried to recall if I had left anything out and wondered if I had failed to answer any of the questions they might have had or were too shocked to ask. As I turned into the driveway, I could see from the light coming from the garage that the back door was open and, as usual, Sylvia was waiting for me.

"How did the pre-op talk go?" she asked, knowing that I was apprehensive about this case.

"It went all right. Things were a little shaky at first, but by the time I finished they seemed to accept everything. They are very nice people. I can't help but feel close to both of them."

"How many bypasses?"

"We looked at the films again tonight, and I still think he needs seven."

"Seven! There have only been a couple of times you've had to do that many."

"Yes, I know. But his risk is greater if I don't bypass all the blockages than if I do."

"Why does he need so many?"

"Well, he has a terrible family history of heart disease. In addition, he's a heavy smoker. He had his first heart attack when he was thirty-three. This is fairly typical of a smoker with a strong family history of heart disease. They always develop blockages at a much younger age."

"You really think smoking has that much to do with it?"

"No question about it. Of the next one hundred consecutive open-hearts we'll do, ninety-five of them will be smokers. We rarely do this operation on nonsmokers."

After eating a light snack, Sylvia and I went out on the deck. We sat in silence. Sylvia was attuned to the fact that there were times when I did not want to talk. At such times she sat as a silent companion, allowing me the freedom of quiet thought.

Later she told me that she was reminiscing about another night on the deck. That was the night before my first open-heart operation after entering private practice four years ago. Out of sheer excitement and nervousness, we had sat on the deck discussing that first case until almost two in the morning. When I finally thought I was sleepy enough to try going to bed, we had gone back into the bedroom. While I was putting on my pajamas, I put one foot through the pee hole. We had both laughed so hard that tears came. Here was a cardiovascular surgeon, preparing to do his first open-heart operation, and he couldn't even get into his pj's. With the tension broken, we both went to bed and slept soundly.

Tonight was different, and Sylvia was aware of it. She wasn't sure exactly what it was, but suspected that it had something to do with the fact that Walter was only two years older than I.

Even Gretchen, our German shepherd, sensed my need for solitude. After receiving a pat on the head and a short rub behind the ears, she went to a comfortable spot a few feet away and did not continue to beg for attention.

Sylvia had taught school during my ten years of medical school, internship, and residency. After I entered practice, with Monte and Gary in school, she began to do volunteer work. Eventually, she expressed a desire to become more involved with what I was doing. She asked to work in the office on a part-time basis, but what started out as part-time help, soon evolved into full-time work. She is now receptionist, secretary, and book-keeper, as well as office manager. To be exact, she runs the entire office, and Julie is our only other employee.

"This one really worries me," I said finally. "It's going to be hard as hell to face Becky if Walter doesn't make it. These cases where young families are involved bother me the most. If I don't get him through it tomorrow, I not only make Becky a widow, but I also leave two young children without a father."

This morning in church Sylvia had noticed that I had kept my head bowed longer than usual after the silent prayer. But until now, she had not perceived the depth of my concern. Through her involvement with patients in the office, she had become much more aware of the deep personal bond between me and my patients and their families.

I got up and stretched. "Well, let's give it a try. I'm not really sleepy but I am pretty tired." It was a little after eleven. In some ways Sylvia almost dreaded going to bed at this time, knowing full well that I would not fall asleep for at least another forty-five minutes to an hour. In spite of how tired I was, she knew that I would toss and turn from the anxiety and apprehension about tomorrow.

After calling the answering service and making sure there were no messages, I placed my beeper in its overnight charger. I turned out the bedside lamp and rolled into bed. I closed my eyes in an effort to say a short prayer for Walter and his family. My thoughts began to drift toward the events that would begin in seven or eight hours. I visualized Walter's coronary arteriograms, trying to fix them in my mind so I would know the exact position and relationship of each of the seven bypass sites. Later, I dreamed I was having difficulty finding and dissecting out the extremely small coronary arteries even with the binocular-type glasses I wore for this part of the operation. Still later, I woke up and went through the nightmarish ritual of performing the operation over and over.

The alarm barely rang before I squelched it. It was Monday, 5:15 A.M. Even though I had gotten less than four hours of sleep, I felt refreshed and looked forward to the day's challenges.

I dressed in a conservative suit, retrieved my beeper, and headed down the hall toward the kitchen. Sylvia had brought me cinnamon toast and coffee while I was dressing, and now I downed a glass of instant breakfast. Whenever I had major surgery scheduled, I had a marked suppression of appetite commensurate with the magnitude of the case involved. As a result, on days when I did open-heart surgery, I ate essentially nothing until that night.

There was very little traffic for the eight miles from our home to St. John's. This early in the morning the deserted streets provided an excellent opportunity for quiet thought and introspection. The bright orange ball of fire in the east was just clearing the horizon. I wondered if Walter were seeing the same sunrise and hoped that Becky was watching it with him. I experienced a sudden feeling of nausea when it struck me that this could be the last sunrise Walter and Becky might ever witness together. As I accelerated onto the freeway, I became determined that this last thought would not come true.

My mind turned now from Walter and Becky to other thoughts—namely, last week's cases. There had been no problems with any of them when I had made rounds last night. I always make thorough rounds each morning before going into surgery because I know that my availability to patients is severely limited when I am in the OR. This is probably the greatest drawback to solo practice. The thing I fear most is being in surgery with a long, complicated case, and having one of my patients "go bad" when I cannot be there. I have worked out a system with one of the other cardiovascular surgeons to help if such a situation should ever arise.

The parking lot behind my office building was empty except for Julie's car. I chose my routine parking place and went into the hospital. When the elevator doors opened to the tenth floor I went directly to Walter's room. The door was slightly ajar, and I knocked before entering. My digital watch read 6:05.

"Good morning, you two." Becky and Walter were sitting on the side of the bed facing the window.

"We were just watching the sunrise," Becky said. "It was simply beautiful."

"I feel great," Walter said. "I'm ready to get this show on the road. You do your part, Tex. I promise to do mine. I'll be the best patient you ever had."

Taking Walter's right hand in both of mine, I gripped it firmly. In that gesture, all of the unspoken hopes and fears we shared were conveyed to each other. "I'll see you downstairs in a little while," I said.

I hugged Becky and whispered in her ear, "I promise to take good care of him."

There was a soft knock and Julie appeared. She had already spent ten minutes with Walter and Becky before I had arrived. She had just missed me as she had gone to check on Walter's pre-op antibiotics and i.v. fluids.

"We'll take good care of you, Walter," Julie said affectionately. The concern expressed in her voice left no doubt that she was sincere. Julie is an excellent surgical technician, but most families do not remember her in that role. What they do remember is her warm smile and comforting manner.

"Okay, Walter," I said, "you better smile this afternoon when we bring Becky in to see you after surgery or I'll kick the hell out of your bed!"

Walter chuckled. "Don't worry about that. I will, no matter how bad I feel!"

5

IT WAS 7:35. The atmosphere in the Surgical Dressing Room was normal for an early Monday morning. Laughter and loud voices filled the room as the anesthesiologists and surgeons shared the new jokes they had heard on tennis courts and golf courses during the weekend. A few physicians discussed current events, focusing especially on gasoline prices and inflation.

Deep in thought about my case and not participating in the discussions, I changed quickly into a white scrub suit. After donning a cap and mask, I headed toward OR 16, the Open-Heart Room.

Julie was already there, holding Walter's hand. During her experience as a circulating nurse in an operating room she had seen how little time the personnel were able to spend with the patients as they lay, almost unnoticed, on the OR table. She always made a special point of coming to the holding area and then to the OR with our patients in order to minimize their feelings of aloneness. She explained the equipment and what each individual person was doing. More important, she reaffirmed the bond that had developed between herself and the patient during the pre-op talk. For this reason, Julie was present at every pre-op talk. Only when the patient could sense that Julie understood what he or she was up against could Julie be truly supportive.

She also knew that the few minutes prior to being put to sleep were not only filled with apprehension and anxiety, but were often perceived by the patients as being their last precious minutes of life. Many patients told her later how much they valued holding her hand and hearing her comforting voice as they began to lose consciousness.

"Hi, Walter, did you do what you were supposed to do when I came through the door?"

"I would have, Tex, if I had seen you come in." There was a sleepy grin on Walter's face. The Demerol was beginning to take effect; he was having difficulty keeping his eyes open.

Julie put Walter's right hand on the arm board in preparation for placing the plastic catheter in his wrist artery so his blood pressure could be measured throughout the surgery. I checked with the pump technicians—Bill, Ron, and Rick—and gave final approval for the drugs to be added to the pump solution.

I then went into a small adjoining room to look at Walter's coronary arteriogram one last time. I wanted to review the exact coronary artery anatomy, the position of each blockage, and the sites where each individual bypass graft would be sutured into place. These pictures had flashed through my mind repeatedly over the past twelve hours, but I familiarized myself with them once again. Any time wasted searching for the vessels to be bypassed would only increase Walter's risk because it would have to be done while his heart was stopped and without blood supply.

The small coronary arteries lie in the fat on the outer surface of the heart. Therefore, it is not necessary to enter the heart to sew in the bypass grafts. Theoretically, open-heart surgery refers to those cases in which it is necessary to actually open a heart chamber or the aorta in order to replace one of the heart valves or repair a birth defect. When I use the term *open-heart surgery*, I am referring to any operation where it is necessary to put the patient on the heart-lung machine and have it completely take over the function of the patient's own heart and lungs.

Finding the minute coronary arteries is not always an easy task. Sometimes they are buried deep in the fatty tissue or the superficial layers of heart muscle. Not only are these vessels difficult to find, but often the exact location of the blockages within the arteries are never seen at the time of surgery. For this reason, complete and accurate recall of the coronary arteriograms is so important.

The heart is relatively fixed in the chest cavity by the large veins and arteries entering and leaving it. Only in the case of heart transplantation is the heart actually removed from the chest cavity. All other types of cardiac surgery are performed without removing the heart. It is simply retracted or tipped on its side to gain adequate exposure of the coronary arteries on its underside. This often necessitates surgeons working in an awkward and sometimes upside-down position in relation to the heart's normal anatomy.

Returning to the main part of OR 16, I picked up the special magnifying glasses that I wore during the delicate part of the operation and checked their final adjustment. After carefully replacing them in their small black box, I moved to Walter's side. "Walter, we're going to put the i.v. in your artery. I told you about this last night. It will hurt, but I will deaden the area as best I can."

Walter turned to watch as I painted his wrist orange with an antiseptic solution and draped the area with sterile towels. After infiltrating the skin with Xylocaine, I slowly inserted a large needle, sheathed in a plastic cannula, into the artery. As I punctured the artery, Walter flinched. Bright red blood began to pulsate from the hub of the needle. I carefully advanced the plastic outer cannula into the artery as the steel inner needle was removed. The cannula was now attached to a pressure monitor.

"Tex, the blood pressure is one hundred eighteen over seventy-four," one of the pump technicians said.

I looked up at the anesthesiologist and nodded. As he placed a black mask over Walter's nose and mouth, he reassured him that it was only oxygen and instructed him to take slow, deep breaths. Walter obeyed without hesitation and gripped Julie's hand.

The room became quiet as all eyes turned toward the anesthesiologist and Walter. As the seconds ticked by, more drugs were infused into the i.v. lines leading to Walter's left arm, speeding on their merciful mission to relieve him of any further anxiety or pain.

Within minutes Walter's grip on Julie's hand relaxed and became flaccid. The anesthesiologist completed the induction of anesthesia by placing a large plastic tube through Walter's mouth into his windpipe. The tube was connected to the anesthetic machine, and vital oxygen as well as the gaseous anesthestic agents flowed into his lungs. His chest rose rhythmically with each inflation.

Walter's head was then turned to the left, and his neck was exposed. After prepping and draping, I passed a large needle into the vein in his neck. I threaded a smaller plastic cannula through this needle into the right atrium of his heart to measure the filling pressure.

Laura, our circulating nurse, placed a rubber catheter through Walter's penis into his bladder and connected it to a drainage bag. This enabled us to measure his kidney function throughout the operation. Then Laura began the long and somewhat tedious process of prepping all areas of skin that would be in the operative field.

Julie and I could now safely leave the operating room to begin our scrub. Before scrubbing, we placed the first of the five promised calls to Becky.

"Walter's asleep," I told her. "We have all of the tubes in. His blood pressure went up a little when we placed the tube in his windpipe, but that's not unusual, and it's now back to normal. His heartbeat has been regular. It will take Julie and me about twenty minutes to wash our hands, put on the drapes, and finally make an incision. It's almost eight fifteen. We should be making an incision around eight thirty-five. It then takes us roughly two hours to take the vein from his leg and get him on the heart-lung machine. When we get on the pump, I will have the nurse call and let you know how we are doing."

"Thanks, Tex. I'm depending on you and Julie to take good care of Walter."

"We'll do the best we can. Keep your chin up. Things will go well."

After that first call, a hospital volunteer offered Becky a cup of coffee. As she drank it, she glanced at her watch and wondered how she was going to make it through the rest of the day. Only three minutes had passed since my call. Becky remembered the hours she had waited for news from the Operating Room during her mother's gall-bladder surgery fifteen years before, and recalled how those hours had seemed like days.

Others in the Waiting Room, anxious for word about their loves ones, looked at her sympathetically. People in these circumstances become acquainted rapidly, and hardly a person in that room was unaware that Becky's husband was undergoing open-heart surgery.

In the Scrub Room located next to OR 16, running water splattered as it struck the stainless-steel sink. Neither Julie nor I spoke. She was reviewing each of the innumerable steps she would be required to perform as my assistant. I was trying to prepare myself for any sudden crisis that might arise.

I peered through the small window in the door between the Scrub Room and OR 16 to check that all was well on the monitors. As I turned back to the sink, my eyes met Julie's. The concern felt by both of us was communicated silently. She knew she should not say anything during these last few minutes, unless she had a very specific question pertaining to the case. Just as I felt that it was crucial to get the patient mentally and emotionally ready for surgery pre-operatively, so I felt that it was equally important that we be prepared.

When I had rinsed the last of the antiseptic soap from my hands, I turned toward Julie. A smile was hidden beneath my mask as I said, "Good luck, Julie."

"Good luck to you, Tex."

As we re-entered Room 16 Laura was beginning to apply the final coating of antiseptic solution from chin to toes to the naked body lying motionless on the OR table. Walter looked grotesque. There was a large plastic tube, over a half inch in diameter, protruding out of his mouth from his windpipe. His eyes were taped shut to protect them from the overhanging tubing that connected the breathing tube to the anesthetic machine. He appeared to have no arms; they were tucked at his side and were covered by a gray sheet. There was a small dressing applied to the i.v. in his neck vein.

At this stage, it was easy for most OR personnel to depersonalize Walter. They did not know him and had had no opportunity to get to know him. But for Julie and me, seeing Walter in this helpless state served as an even greater reminder of exactly how much he had entrusted himself to us.

Helen, one of the two surgical technicians, was a true veteran of the OR. She had been scrubbing on open-heart cases at St. John's for over eight years, and to her this was just another case. At least this was the way she appeared on the outside. Inside, Helen was extremely conscientious about each patient. She was an expert at her job. She knew that any delay on her part could jeopardize the patient's life. She anticipated every instrument that I would need. She was good, and she knew it. Her greeting to me was cool, as usual, but under this coolness I knew there was a genuine loyalty coupled with a deep sensitivity toward me.

Helen had played an important part in sustaining me during the initial difficult months of getting my practice started. Loyal and supportive, she never let me down. On innumerable occasions, cases had run past her quitting time, but instead of letting someone who was not used to working with me in the Open-Heart Room come in and relieve her, she stayed until the case was completed.

Pat, the other surgical technician, had joined the open-heart team a few months after I had entered practice. She was usually smiling and enthusiastic, and worked well with Helen. Pat's loyalty to me, like Helen's, was almost as important as the excellence of her technical skills.

Laura, the circulating nurse and a member of the team for over three years, was loved and respected by everyone in the OR. She was extremely efficient and always pleasant. I deeply appreciated the concern and gentleness with which she delivered the messages from the OR to the families.

After being gowned and gloved, Julie stood at Walter's left and I moved to the opposite side. Laura finished the final prep, and we performed the complicated ritual of draping. When it was completed, a great deal of Walter still remained exposed. This included the lower portion of his neck, the front of the chest and abdomen, plus both legs. These areas were then covered with sterile plastic adhesive drapes.

Helen and Pat readied the rest of the field for the operation. They brought up the pump lines, attached the sucker tubing, and dropped the cautery cord off the sterile field and Laura connected it to an electric machine. The cautery would be used to coagulate, or burn, small blood vessels to stop the bleeding during the operation.

I picked up a scalpel and unceremoniously made a small two-inch incision over Walter's right ankle. I looked up at the clock and saw that it was 8:25. Already we were ten minutes ahead of schedule. Using great care not to injure the vein, I extended the incision from Walter's right ankle to his groin area. By 8:45, the vein had been removed and each individual branch had been clamped and tied with fine silk suture. Based on the times that I had given Becky, I was now almost an hour ahead of schedule. This would give me some leeway should problems arise while getting Walter on the pump.

At 8:35, Becky had looked at her watch and announced, "Well, I guess they've started by now. Despite the reassurances she received from her pastor and several close friends, a feeling of empathy for Walter overwhelmed her as she realized the first incision was being made. Both hands tightly clutched the cup of coffee from which she had taken only a few sips. She finally relaxed her grip ever so slightly. She realized that according to what I had told her, the next hour should be spent removing the vein. Then the most important part of the operation would begin.

Julie moved from the leg to the chest area, anticipating the next step. I was a little slower in taking my position. I moved cautiously in order to avoid stepping on the lines that extended from the heart-lung machine to Walter's side, where they had been tightly secured. Pat assumed her position and began the tedious process of closing the long leg incision. Without saying a word, I extended my hand toward Helen and she carefully placed a scalpel in it.

The long skin incision was made from the top of the sternum, to a point a third of the way between the sternum and the navel. The bleeding was stopped by use of the coagulating cautery. A small saw, which looked much like a jig saw, was used to divide the breastbone. After bleeding from the sternum was stopped, a large retractor was placed between the edges of the split sternum. This was used to jack open the chest cavity nine to ten inches.

Upon opening the sternum there was a slight drop in Walter's blood pressure to ninety-six over sixty-eight. Although concerned, I knew this was not unusual. Up to this point I felt more like a "bone doctor" than a cardiovascular surgeon. It always seemed to take more time to get through the sternum and contol the bleeding than to complete the remaining steps necessary to place the patient on the heart-lung machine. The pericardium, or heart sac, was now opened and retracted. For the first time we could see Walter's beating heart. Swiftly, but precisely, sutures were placed in the aorta, as well as in the right atrium. The only sounds in the room were the slap of instruments into my gloved hand as Helen correctly anticipated every move. Having placed two large plastic cannulas in the right atrium and another into the aorta, I addressed the pump team. "Are you guys ready?"

Upon receiving an affirmative answer, I removed the clamps from the two cannulas in the right atrium. "Let's go." It was eight minutes after nine.

It took only five minutes for the chilled solution entering Walter's body from the heart-lung machine to cause his heart to fibrillate. When his heart fibrillated, it stopped pumping effectively and Walter was now totally dependent on the heart-lung machine.

I placed a clamp across the aorta, completely shutting off any blood supply to his heart. A large needle was inserted into the aorta between the clamp and the heart itself and a forty-degree solution was infused under pressure into the coronary arteries. This solution cooled the heart muscle even more, protecting it while it was without its blood supply (see Figure 4).

I asked for my special glasses that had the magnifiying lenses attached to them. Bill, the chief pump technician, removed my regular glasses, replacing them with the much heavier magnifying loupes.

The vein that had been removed from Walter's leg was brought up to the chest area. It was distended with blood to enable us to visualize untied branches and other bleeding points. When all of these had been either tied or sewn with very fine suture, I turned my attention back to the heart. I glanced up at the clock and noted that it was 9:17.

"Laura, call Becky at ten o'clock and let her know that we're on the pump." Ten o'clock would be thirty-five minutes ahead of the time that I had projected to Becky for going on the pump. Because there had been no problems or complications with Walter, we were now more than an hour and a half ahead of the schedule I had given her in the pre-op talk.

Pat left her position at the leg and stationed herself at my left. Her job was to hold the heart so that each blocked artery was exposed. She tilted the heart toward Walter's chin to expose the underside. I began to dissect out each of the branches of the coronary arteries that would need bypassing.

The suturing of the vein graft to the first heart artery was then started. Even under my magnifying loupes the heart arteries looked extremely tiny. Their walls were as thin as tissue paper, but this was almost always true. Julie's help was excellent. Pat maintained exposure, and Helen never caused me to wait for a single instrument. Carefully and precisely we completed each of the seven critical bypasses, using suture as fine as hair. As the next to the last bypass was started, the cold solution infusing into the root of the aorta was discontinued. The pump team began to warm the blood returning to Walter's body.

When the suturing of the seventh bypass graft was completed, the clamp across the aorta was removed. For the first time in ninety-one minutes Walter's heart received oxygenated blood—the substance it so desperately needed to survive.

I applied a small electric shock to Walter's heart. Immediately it converted from fibrillation and began to beat with slow rhythmic contractions. I looked up at the monitor to study his electrocardiogram, then glanced at the clock. I was amazed at how rapidly the time had passed. It was 10:42.

Almost forty minutes earlier Becky had been startled out of a conversation with one of her friends when the volunteer at the desk called her name. She walked briskly to the phone, fearing the worst. Her anxiety was further compounded when she heard a nurse's voice instead of mine. Something must have gone wrong, she thought. But Laura's soothing tone reassured her that Walter was on the pump and that everything was going well.

Becky returned to her friends and excitedly reported that I was ahead of schedule. Within minutes the good news had spread around the room. It was then that Becky remembered I had said a nurse would make all of the calls after my initial one.

"That looks better," Julie said, referring to the improvement in the electrocardiogram pattern as the heart responded to the re-establishment of its blood supply.

Walter's heart was now beating more forcefully. I felt more confident that the speed with which the bypasses had been completed would make the difference between his survival and death. There had been a few bad moments while suturing the bypasses to the coronary arteries, when things hadn't gone quite right. Each time I had stamped my foot and exclaimed "Damnit." I was angry at myself for extending the time that Walter's heart was without its blood supply, thereby increasing the risk of heart attack.

Even though Walter's heart was now beating, it was fed by blood flowing through his blocked arteries. The three unattached ends of the vein bypass grafts still had to be connected to the aorta. Only then could they carry their precious cargo to his oxygen-starved heart (see Figure 5).

The aorta was partially occluded with a special clamp, and three holes were made in it. The unattached ends of the bypass grafts were sutured to these holes. The aorta is approximately fifty millimeters, or roughly two inches, in diameter. A normal coronary artery is one to two millimeters in diameter. Therefore, this portion of the procedure of sewing the vein bypass grafts to the aorta proceeded with comparative ease. Upon completion, the clamp was removed and for the first time blood flowed through the bypass grafts to the coronary arteries beyond their blockages. Almost immediately there was a change for the better in the electrocardiogram. The strength of each heartbeat improved with almost every contraction.

"Laura," I said, "you can tell Becky that we're halfway through with the bypass procedure and things are satisfactory." This was all that I wanted Becky to know at present. The difficult part of getting Walter off the pump lay ahead. If we had problems at that time, Becky would be spared the anxiety of wondering what was wrong. If it became obvious that Walter was not going to make it off the pump, several phone calls could be made in a short period to inform Becky of the grim outlook.

The real test of how well we had performed the operation was about to occur. We would come to know whether we would share with Walter and Becky the joy of success, or with Becky alone, the heartbreak of failure.

After rewarming Walter's body to an acceptable temperature, I asked if everyone was ready to try to come off the pump. With no dissensions, I placed clamps across the two plastic tubes coming from the right atrium. "We're off!"

Ron and Rick began to chime out the blood pressure. "Eighty over sixty-two. Eighty-eight over sixty-eight. Ninety-four over seventy-two. One hundred over seventy-six."

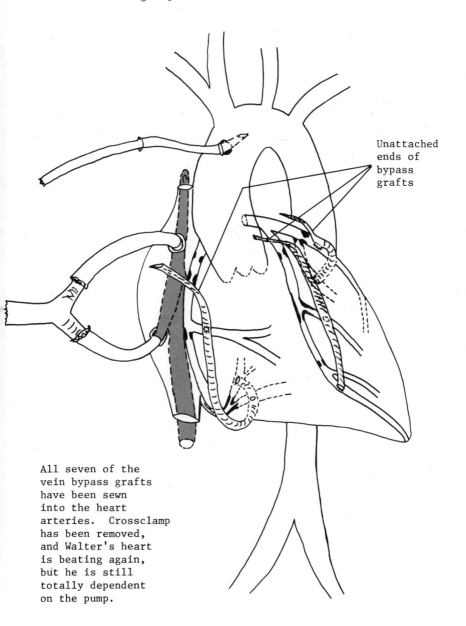

Figure 5 • "Halfway Through"

Unattached
ends of
bypass
grafts

All seven of the
vein bypass grafts
have been sewn
into the heart
arteries. Crossclamp
has been removed,
and Walter's heart
is beating again,
but he is still
totally dependent
on the pump.

The pressure rose steadily as Bill reinfused most of the blood from the pump back into Walter. Bill retained only enough blood to keep his lines primed should I request that we return to the pump's support.

The tension in OR 16 lifted for the first time. The clock read 11:20. There was not a person in the room who was not now involved with Walter, as they were eventually with every open-heart patient. Even though the OR personnel had tried to depersonalize him initially, they were deeply moved when they saw his heart struggle successfully to free itself from the dependency of the pump. As for Julie and me, words could not express the exhilaration we felt.

With mixed emotions, Becky had received Laura's call informing her that we were halfway through. She was thrilled that we were moving along so much more rapidly than she had anticipated, but she knew that the next phone call would be the most critical of all. She almost dreaded being called to the volunteer's desk to receive the next message from the OR.

As she returned to her friends to relay what Laura had told her, she felt her first twinge of confidence. Things seemed to be going so much more smoothly and rapidly than she had expected. There was no way for her to know that Walter was already off the pump and doing well.

Walter's blood pressure was now up to one hundred thirty over eighty-four. All of the cannulas had been removed from the heart and aorta. The stimulating drugs for his heart had been discontinued; he was essentially on his own (see Figure 6).

A drug was being given slowly by the anesthesiologist to reverse the heparin, which had been used to thin Walter's blood so that it would not clot in the heart-lung machine. During this time Julie and I worked to stop all oozing, making sure that all

Figure 6 • OFF THE PUMP!

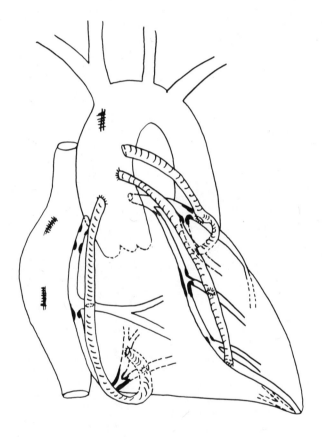

possible sites of potential hemorrhage were checked and re-
checked. When control of the bleeding was satisfactory, I asked
for the chest tubes. "Let's get the hell out of here!"

This was what everyone was waiting for. The pump team
could now begin moving the lines away from the patient and start
cleaning up the equipment. Pat had finished closing the leg and
asked if she could leave for a break, returning later so that Helen
could do the same. Julie stepped back from the table to relieve
the strain on her back.

I removed the retractor from Walter's chest. Although his
blood pressure fell somewhat, this was expected. I resumed my
role as "bone doctor" and began to place heavy stainless-steel
wire sutures through the sternum. After they were all in place,
Julie approximated the edges of the sternum with a special instrument. Each wire was then twisted so as to hold the divided bone
firmly in position for healing. The multiple individual wires were
cut and the remaining tails were bent down so that they would
not protrude through the skin.

It was 12:15, slightly less than four hours since the initial skin
incision had been made. All that remained was to close the muscle and skin of the chest. "Laura, you can tell Becky we're off the
pump. He came off the first time without any problems, and I'm
very pleased with the way things look now."

The phone had been ringing frequently at the information
desk. Various families had received calls to inform them that
their loved one's surgery had been successfully completed. Becky
had no idea that this call would be for her. She half ran to the
phone, and listened nervously. As Laura repeated the message
that I had asked her to deliver, a broad smile broke across Becky's
face. No one observing her doubted what she was being told.

Julie and I finished closing the skin. We helped apply the
dressings over the chest and leg wounds as well as around the

large plastic tubes protruding through Walter's upper abdomen from beneath the sternum. The drapes were removed from his swollen face.

Walter was transferred from the OR table to the ICU bed. The anesthesiologist stood at the head of Walter's bed using a portable oxygen unit to inflate periodically Walter's lungs. A battery-powered monitor echoed every heartbeat. The trip to the ICU began. If anything happened to Walter during the transfer from surgery to the ICU, very little could be done until the distance of several hundred feet had been traversed.

After expressing my appreciation to the pump team, I turned to Julie, Helen, Pat, and Laura and gave each of them a word of thanks. I asked Laura to make the final phone call to Becky. "Tell her that we are closing and it will take one hour and fifteen minutes to close and get Walter settled in the ICU."

Julie and I hurried to catch up with the entourage of anesthesiologist, orderly, and patient. I looked at the clock in the hallway. It was 12:45.

6

THE NURSES in the ICU moved quickly and efficiently to attach Walter's breathing tube to the respirator which would breathe for him while he was still anesthetized. The arterial line, cardiac electrodes, and rectal temperature probe were connected to the monitoring screen located above his bed.

Julie and I finally relaxed when the blood-pressure monitor read one hundred twenty-four over eighty-six. This was what it had been when we left the OR. The electrocardiogram pattern was normal, without any irregular beats. The digital read-out showed a heart rate of ninety-four. Walter's temperature registered 35.6 degrees C. (96.1 F.).

I checked and was satisfied with the amount of urine that had been produced since Walter came off the pump. Its pink-tinged color, indicative of red-blood-cell destruction secondary to the long pump run, was not unusual, though a cause for concern.

The container hanging at the foot of the bed to collect the blood draining from the chest tubes measured 120 cc's, which is equivalent to approximately half a glass of water. This was certainly acceptable at this point. I expected Walter to ooze between 50 and 75 cc's per hour for the first several hours, but then hoped that it would taper off through the rest of the night.

While the initial post-operative chest X-ray and electrocardiogram were being done, the routine blood work was drawn. Julie remained to observe any significant changes in Walter's vital signs, and I went out to the main ICU desk, where I made a progress note about the operative procedure, the findings at surgery, and wrote the post-op orders. I phoned Walter's referring physician to notify him that the surgery had been successfully completed, the post-op electrocardiogram showed no acute injury or damage, and that stimulating drugs were no longer necessary.

I called Sylvia to let her know that Walter was okay. I then began to dictate the detailed operative report, once again retracing each step of the procedure. As I dictated, I recalled the anatomy of Walter's coronary arteries for possibly the last time. This anatomy would soon have to be erased from my memory forever, to be replaced by the new set of coronary arteriograms on the patient I had been asked to see this afternoon.

All cardiovascular surgeons must engage in these mental gymnastics. Prior to surgery, we view and review a set of coronary arteriograms repeatedly until they are committed to memory. After the surgery is over, we have to erase them from our minds completely and concentrate on the next patient's arteriograms.

Julie was waiting as I finished dictating. "He moves both arms and both legs!" she said jubilantly.

For the first time in almost eighteen hours I felt genuinely relieved. Walter had now arrived safely through the three greatest risks that I had so carefully explained to him and Becky. With an enthusiasm that could hardly be contained, I hurried back to his room.

Walter was having intermittent episodes of shivering. He was just beginning to emerge from anesthesia and was aware of the sounds around him—the nurses announcing their findings on physical examination and repeating orders, the noise of the breathing machine, and the bleep of the cardiac monitor.

The large plastic tube that entered his mouth, passing between his vocal cords, caused him to feel a sensation of choking. Every time he started to take a breath, the breathing machine would force air into his lungs. Because this caused pressure on his sternum, he experienced pain in his chest incision. While he remained oblivious to the i.v. lines in his neck, both arms, and in the artery in his right wrist, he was aware of the tubes entering his upper abdomen and extending under the sternum. These initiated significant muscle spasms, which probably caused him the greatest discomfort, other than the plastic tube in his windpipe.

Soon, he felt he needed to urinate and was embarrassed that he might do it in bed. He failed to recall that the rubber catheter in his bladder had a balloon on the end of it, securing it in place and that the catheter would give him a false urge to urinate. All of this faded in and out of Walter's consciousness. He could not quite comprehend what was happening.

Julie bent over the railing of his bed and began to give commands. "Walter, open your eyes for Tex. Wiggle the fingers of your left hand. Now your right. Now both feet."

Walter later said, "I thought an angel from heaven was talking to me. I will never forget the joy I felt when I realized the angel was Julie."

After watching Walter's response to Julie's instructions, I said, "You're in the ICU. Your surgery is over, Walter. We're going to get Becky now. Remember, you better smile when she comes in."

A twisted but definite grin appeared on Walter's face. It was difficult for him to move his lips because tape had been applied to secure the breathing tube. But he had tried!

Walter had been back from surgery for almost an hour. I wanted to be very sure that he was all right before I brought Becky in. I could think of nothing worse than to have a patient suddenly hemorrhage or "go bad" in front of family members. This is most likely to occur during the first hour after surgery.

As Julie and I entered the Waiting Room, all faces turned toward us. Each person was hoping that his or her doctor was bringing news of a loved one. At first Becky did not recognize us, not expecting to see us in scrub clothes. But then she got up quickly and ran to me with arms outstretched. As we clasped hands and I told her how pleased I was with Walter's progress, she could no longer suppress her emotions. Flinging her arms around me, and then around Julie, she tried to hold back tears of joy.

"Walter came off the pump exceptionally well," I explained. "There is no evidence of heart damage. We were able to do all seven bypasses. He's bleeding minimally. The best news of all is that there is no evidence of stroke."

With a deep sigh, Becky turned to her minister, who had waited with her through the surgery. "Thank you so much for your help. You said he'd be okay, and you were right."

"Becky," I said, "I guess you could tell that we were quite a bit ahead of the time frame that I gave you last night."

"Yes, we just couldn't believe how rapidly it went."

"The times I gave you were deliberately, but realistically, extended to allow for any difficulties that might have arisen during surgery. Sometimes it takes as long as I told you. If you expect it to take a long time and it doesn't, then that's great. But once in a while we run into problems, and it's better if you're prepared. The calls were one step behind what as actually happening in the operating room. When we called to tell you that we were on the pump, we had been on the pump for almost forty-five minutes. When we called to tell you we were halfway through, we were already off the pump. When we called to tell you we were off the pump, we were beginning to close." I couldn't help smiling as I said, "Our last call, to inform you we were closing, was made as we were moving Walter to the ICU. Walter has been in the ICU for over an hour. He's doing fine."

"You really had me fooled," Becky admitted. We expected

the surgery to take six or seven hours after what you told us last night."

"If you're ready, we'll take you to see Walter. I would prefer that only immediate family members go in to the ICU. The first visit is more for your benefit than for Walter's. He has a tube in his windpipe, and it will be very frustrating for him not to be able to talk to you. This visit is just to let you see that he is okay. I may have exaggerated the time that surgery would take, but everything else is exactly as I said it would be. He will have all the tubes and look just as bad as I told you he would."

It had been easy for Becky to walk into one of the ICU rooms last night when Julie had brought her down. But now she approached Walter's room with some trepidation, glad to have me on one side and Julie supporting her other arm.

"Let's stop here," I said as we reached the doorway. "At the end of the bed you can see the container into which the chest tubes are draining. There has been less than two hundred cc's of bleeding since the operation. That is equivalent to a little less than a glass of water, and is quite acceptable. The monitor over Walter's head shows his blood pressure to be one hundred eighteen over seventy-four and his pulse is eighty-two, both of which are normal. His temperature is now thirty-six point two degrees centigrade, which is ninety-seven point two degrees Fahrenheit.

"The large blue machine with the flashing amber light is the breathing machine. When the light comes on, it means that Walter is triggering the breath and the machine is just helping him."

Becky was having a hard time concentrating on what I was saying. Her attention was fixed on Walter's face—pale, swollen, and distorted by the tube in his mouth and the tape holding it in place.

When we reached the bedside, Becky put her hand on his shoulder, leaned down, and said, "Walter, it's me."

Walter opened his eyes.

"Honey, it's all over. Get some rest. I'll see you later."

Walter nodded slowly, careful not to increase the discomfort of the tube. He was unable to utter a sound, but gave Becky's hand a gentle squeeze. The only thing he would recall from this first hour after surgery was Julie's command to wiggle his fingers and his toes.

"He didn't look as bad as you said he was going to," Becky said as we left the room.

"Then we did a good job of preparing you. If he had looked worse than you expected, then I would feel that I had let you down. We're not completely out of the woods, but we're probably ninety-five percent of the way through the bad things. If he doesn't start hemorrhaging in the next hour or so, I think we have it made. I'd like for you to stay in the Waiting Room or in the cafeteria so I can find you if there are any problems. I'll see you again several times this afternoon. I just want to know exactly where you are."

As we left the ICU Becky began to sob, finally able to release her tension. Julie comforted her and told her that it was okay to cry.

"I'm crying because I'm *happy*, not because I'm upset," Becky said. "I'm just glad it's over."

7

A T THE OFFICE, Sylvia wanted to hear about the morning. Now Julie and I could fill her in on the details of the surgery and how Walter and Becky were doing.

Among the messages on my desk were two additional requests for consultations other than the one I had already received in the OR. The earlier consult concerned a man in his early forties with pre-infarction angina, or severe heart pain, but without definite evidence of a heart attack. He had been cathed this morning and urgently needed bypass surgery. The two other consultations were on a sixty-eight-year-old woman and a fifty-seven-year-old man who had undergone coronary artery bypass surgery eight years ago. He had developed new blockages and was in need of being reoperated. I had Julie call and tentatively schedule these cases for Tuesday, Wednesday, and Thursday, respectively.

After being off our feet for a little while, I indicated to Julie that we had better get back to the hospital to check on Walter and start seeing the consults if we wanted to get home before midnight.

Walter had begun to emerge from the anesthesia. Fully conscious, he responded easily to commands and winked at Julie as she took his hand. He tried to smile at me but couldn't because of the mass of tape that held his breathing tube in place.

"Your surgery is over and you're fine, Walter. You're in the ICU."

I feel it is very important to keep reassuring the patients that they are out of surgery and all is going well since patients coming out from under anesthesia are likely to have one of several inappropriate reactions. Many ask, "When am I going to have surgery?" In this case, we simply tell the patients that they have come through surgery and are in the ICU. Other patients, because of the surgically induced chest pain, express fear that a heart attack has occurred and the surgery has been postponed. This anxiety is more difficult to handle. It requires a careful explanation that surgery is over and the pain is incisional, not the pain of a heart attack. In part, this problem is a result of my pre-op talk in which I discuss the possibility that a heart attack can occur as patients are put to sleep.

I disconnected the respirator from Walter's breathing tube and placed my hand over it to assess the depth of the breaths he was able to take. After having him take several breaths, I asked, "Are you getting enough air? Can you breathe easier without the machine than with it?" Walter nodded his head up and down. When I was satisfied that he was taking deep enough breaths, I said, "Let's put him on flow-by oxygen for fifteen minutes, and see how he does on his own. If his blood gases are okay, we'll pull the tube out of his windpipe."

I believe in early removal of the breathing tube for several reasons. First, most patients complain that it is the worst part of their post-op experience. It is frightening for them not to be able to communicate in a normal manner. Second, I feel that if God wanted people to breathe through a plastic tube, He would have made us that way, and He didn't.

During my residency I had been trained to keep the tube in patients and leave them on a breathing machine for the first twenty-four hours post-op. But my first open-heart surgery patient in private practice had caused me to re-evaluate this aspect of my training. This patient, Jerry, contributed immeasurably to the way in which I now manage my open-heart patients post-operatively. He had been extremely apprehensive, and I had spent a great deal of time with him prior to surgery. By the day of surgery he was so emotionally primed that he would, and could, do anything I asked of him. Within four hours after surgery he was breathing very well on his own and had written a note asking if the breathing tube could be removed. I checked the blood gases and, having found them to be excellent, removed the tube. He had no breathing problems thereafter and a precedent for early removal of the breathing tube on my open-heart patients had been set.

Jerry's next request, within six hours after surgery, was that he be allowed to get off his back. I let him sit up on the edge of the bed. He tolerated this so well that standing him at the bedside followed naturally. I stood him up and was pleasantly surprised to find that the standing position greatly relieved the discomfort of the abdominal muscle spasms associated with the chest tubes. During the next twenty-four hours, I never left Jerry's side. Since this was my first patient, I didn't want anything to happen to him. Being nervous about how rapidly he was progressing, I felt I should be present and take full responsibility. Having seen for myself how well Jerry did, I made it a practice to stand my open-heart patients at the bedside several times during the first night after surgery.

The morning after surgery all tubes and lines were removed, and I walked Jerry the full length of the ICU. As we walked, the nurses applauded. The louder they applauded, the faster Jerry walked. He was, without a doubt, the healthiest patient in the ICU and no longer needed to be there. So, I transferred him to the post-op surgical floor, much to the surprise of the nursing staff. The nurses on the floor to which he was assigned had had no experience with a patient who was only one day post-op from open-heart surgery. Most patients were three or more days post-op when this floor received them. However, the nurses quickly learned to provide exactly the kind of care that was needed, and Jerry did extremely well under their watchful eyes.

Several days later, after seeing Jerry four or five times a day, I said, "I have a confession to make to you."

"What do you mean?" His reaction was almost paranoid.

"You called me the week before you came to the hospital and asked if I had done many operations like yours. I told you that I had. That was the truth, but they were all done during my training in residency. You are the first open-heart patient that I have operated upon in private practice."

"Is that right?" Jerry exclaimed. "You know, I didn't understand why all the nurses and everyone around the hospital were so surprised by how well I did. You would think they were looking at a freak. But now it makes sense. Remember when you would come over and spend time with me, getting me up and walking me in the halls? When you left, some of the nurses came back to my room and asked, 'Who was that guy that was walking with you?' I answered, 'Well, that's Tex. He's my doctor. Don't you know him?' I was surprised that they were even asking the question. Now I understand why."

The situation was different today. Walter would face many anxious moments, but at least he would not have to go through the anxiety of being my first patient in private practice, and the nurses would know who his doctor was.

The results of the blood gases returned and were excellent. I decided to pull the tube from Walter's windpipe. "Are you ready to get rid of that breathing tube?" Despite the limitations of the tape, Walter managed a big grin. "This is going to make you cough," I cautioned, "and will hurt like hell as I pull the tube. Bear with me and we'll get it out."

Taking a small plastic suction catheter, I passed it down the breathing tube, and as Walter coughed I removed the tube. At the same time I applied suction to the catheter to remove the mucus that had accumulated in his windpipe. For a moment it was difficult for Walter to get his breath. Then he coughed up the mucus that had gathered in the back of his throat and began to breathe well on his own for the first time in more than eight hours.

"Boy, that damn tube hurts like hell!" Walter exclaimed. "I hope you don't have to put it back in!"

"We won't have to as long as you cough, but if you don't cough and begin getting in trouble with pneumonia, we'll have to replace it. You have a choice. Cough, even though it hurts, or you get that tube put back down your windpipe."

Walter responded with a feeble cough that got better with each effort. Then, very seriously, he asked, "How did I do this morning?"

"Just great. You came off the pump the first time and we were able to do all seven bypasses."

"Has Becky been in? Did she take it okay?" Walter asked.

"She was hesitant at first, but then she adjusted to all the tubes and the initial fright. She really thought you looked very good."

"When can I see her again?" he asked.

"It's almost four o'clock. She can see you again in about an hour and a half. We'll let her know that we've taken the tube out of your windpipe. And, Walter, don't forget my rule when she comes in."

"You don't have to worry about that!" Walter said.

After listening to his heart and lungs, I wrote a brief progress note as well as orders for oral pain medications and liquids as desired. Then Julie and I went to the Waiting Room. Knowing that the expression on our faces would reveal much of the story we had to tell, we always made it a point to be cheerful as we entered.

"Is Walter still doing as well as when I saw him before?" Becky asked.

"Yes, he is. We already have the tube out of his windpipe and he is breathing on his own. Everything is going according to plan."

After reporting in more detail, Julie and I left to view the coronary arteriograms on our three consults. We then visited the woman in her late sixties and the man in his fifties. Both were agreeable to surgery, and we set up a time convenient for them and their families for the pre-op talk. Our next stop was the Coronary Care Unit (CCU) on the eighth floor to visit with John, the most critical of the three, whom we had scheduled for surgery the following morning.

John had come to the Emergency Room with severe chest pain five days earlier and had been admitted directly to the CCU because of the possibility of a heart attack. Subsequently, multiple electrocardiograms as well as blood tests were performed and no evidence of heart damage was found. Therefore it was felt that John's heart pain was preinfarction angina—warning of an impending heart attack. This morning he had undergone a cardiac catheterization to determine the extent of blockages.

John, an aggressive executive, was forty-two years old and the father of three children, all of whom were either in college or high school. He had resisted coming to the hospital because he initially thought his discomfort was only indigestion. The urgent pleas of his wife, Mary, coupled with the development of a cold, clammy sweat and onset of severe chest pain finally persuaded him to come to the Emergency Room. After a heart attack had been ruled out, he was extremely reluctant to undergo a heart cath and did so because of the insistence of Mary and close friends who knew people who had suffered severe heart attacks at his age. It was still difficult for him to understand why he needed further tests, especially something as extensive as a heart cath. He had even threatened to leave St. John's Sunday night, insisting that he was okay. Only after much persuasion from his family physician, who was also a close personal friend, did he agree to stay.

Julie and I reviewed John's chart in detail and soon learned that he had been a difficult patient for the nurses. He had refused to follow instructions about keeping his oxygen on and had been generally uncooperative. He had continually complained about the food and about being unable to smoke. We had had experience with patients like this and knew what we were up against.

Once the introductions had been completed and all of us, including Mary and their three children, were seated in John's CCU room, I proceeded to describe the findings from John's heart cath. As I completed the drawing, I described the various alternatives: doing nothing, medical management, or surgery. Since two of John's main arteries were 90 percent blocked, I felt strongly that he should undergo bypass surgery. His history of occasional chest discomfort for the last four to six weeks after even minimal exercise further strengthened my opinion that surgery was needed.

Mary was a perceptive person, as were the children. They quickly realized that John had no real choice; the only sensible thing was to undergo bypass surgery. John, on the other hand, continued to argue his point that he was now doing very well, was not having pain, and could not understand why he needed surgery.

"John, you have critical blockages in two of your main heart arteries. Sometime down the line you're going to have a heart attack. I don't know when that will be. He does," I said, as I pointed skyward. "When you have a heart attack, the area of heart muscle that dies is lost forever and turns into scar tissue.

We want to prevent that from happening. You should feel very fortunate that you at least had some warning. Your first sign of heart disease was chest pain rather than a heart attack."

Finally, John agreed to go ahead with surgery, albeit reluctantly. We spent the next hour going over the risks involved, where the family should wait, how long John would be in the ICU, and all of the other details, just as we had done the evening before with Walter. There was a marked difference between John's attitude and that of Walter. John's hostility erected a barrier against any psychological and emotional preparation that Julie and I attempted to achieve. His attitude was so negative that I would probably have postponed the surgery had I not felt so strongly that he was in extreme danger of having a heart attack. The fact that he had had angina this morning following his heart cath was of tremendous concern to me.

Mary and the children, on the other hand, were receptive and appreciative. They were glad that John had finally made the decision to go ahead, but were also aware of his reluctance. They seemed to fully understand the risks involved.

As usual, I ended the pre-op talk by being sure that John understood my two rules. He agreed, but I had my doubts that he would follow them.

Julie and I realized that our pre-op talk had not accomplished all that we hoped it would with John, but were heartened that we had established rapport with Mary and the children. This was very important to us. We would be able to help them if things did not go as we hoped they would tomorrow.

Julie then spoke to Mary and the children, "If you'll wait here, I'll come back in a little while to show you where the Surgical Waiting Room is and take you to see the ICU. I'll let you see the young man we did open-heart surgery on this morning. You'll get an idea of how John will look tomorrow at this time."

I added, "We did seven bypasses on him, not just two as we

are going to do on you, John. He's ready to get up, and I expect the same performance from you."

John recognized this challenge for what it was and replied, "Well, if he can do it, I suppose I can too." This response was still far from the fighting spirit I so much wanted him to display.

"Boy, he has one of the worst attitudes I've seen in a long time," I said to Julie as we left the CCU.

"You're really worried about him, aren't you?"

"You watch! He'll do fine from a surgical standpoint; I'm not worried about that. His risk is probably less than three percent because he's so young. I'm much more concerned about his attitude afterward. He'll be extremely hard to motivate and will be the type of person who will refuse to do anything we ask of him. He'll probably be off work for months when he really doesn't need to be. I've seen this type before; I dread operating on them. If his blockages weren't so tight, I would recommend that he wait until he has a much more positive attitude toward surgery. All we can do is our job and hope for the best."

8

LEAVING THE CCU, we went directly to the ICU, where Walter greeted us with, "I feel as though that safe is sitting on my chest, but don't get me wrong—I'm glad I'm here. Where have you all been? You said you were going to get me up around five and it's almost six thirty!"

"That's the attitude we prayed you would have, Walter," I said. "I'm sorry, but we were seeing consults and giving a pre-op talk to the patient for open-heart surgery tomorrow. I apologize for not being here earlier." By this time I was gripping Walter's outstretched right hand, somewhat restrained by the line in his artery. Our grip now signified a true bond of friendship, rather than one of hope, as had been the case the night before.

At the opposite side of the bed Julie took his left hand. "You look great, Walter. You really did super this morning!"

I listened to Walter's heart with my stethoscope and heard the usual sound with every beat, created by the rubbing of the heart against its sac. After having him take some deep breaths and satisfied that he was exchanging air, I said, "Your lungs are fairly clear and your heart sounds good. Are you ready to get up?"

"I told you, I was ready to get up an hour ago. I was disappointed it took you this long to get back."

Julie began to move the tubes and lines to the side of Walter's bed in preparation for standing him while I elevated the head of the bed. Leaning over him, I directed, "Put both arms around my neck, and I'll pull you up. Don't move suddenly. Let me pull you up." Walter obeyed, and with Julie guiding his feet over the side of the bed, I straightened up and pulled him with me, supporting his head and back with my arms. Bringing him up to a sitting position, almost in a single motion, we moved from sitting to standing. I had learned that sitting was very uncomfortable for the patient because of the abdominal muscle spasms caused by the chest tubes.

"This is hard to believe," Walter exclaimed. "Twelve hours ago I was wondering if I would see another sunrise and now here I am, standing up only six hours after surgery."

I monitored the small TV screen above Walter's bed to be sure that his blood pressure was staying at an acceptable level and that he was having no irregularities of his heart beat. Satisfied that he was stable, I asked, "Are you dizzy?" Walter shook his head no. "Don't just shake your head; talk to me. It makes me nervous when you don't talk. I worry that something is wrong. How does it feel to be off your back?"

"It actually feels pretty good. I was getting tired of lying in bed. But the worst thing was that damn tube in my windpipe. It was frustrating not to be able to tell people that you needed to pee or that you needed something for pain. Your nurses were great at figuring out what I was trying to say, but it was still frustrating."

"Are you getting enough air?"

"I'm getting plenty of air. Besides, I wouldn't tell you if I wasn't. You might put that tube back down my windpipe."

"Well, you cough Walter or I will put the tube back. Cough, and I mean now! Take this pillow and hug it tightly against your chest. I want to hear a good cough."

Walter clutched the pillow against his chest incision and

made an effort to cough.

"That wasn't worth a damn! I told you that I wasn't going to let you get pneumonia. So here goes."

I took a small catheter, similar to the one I had placed down Walter's breathing tube when I had removed it, and put it through his nose into the back of his throat. Gently I began to advance it into the windpipe. The catheter immediately caused multiple vigorous coughs.

"All right, that's enough for now. Take a few deep breaths and then we'll do it one more time." The tears in Walter's eyes showed that the deep coughs had produced pain. "I'm sorry, Walter. I know that hurt," I said apologetically, "but I told you we weren't going to have trouble with your lungs, and I tried to warn you about smoking before surgery. You will cough every hour or so and you will do it on your own and do it well, or I'll put this catheter through your nose into your windpipe many more times before you leave St. John's."

Walter managed a grin as he wiped the tears away. "I told you that if you did your part I would be your best patient, and I won't let you down."

I was sorry to put him through the pain and discomfort of making him cough, but I knew it was for his benefit. I was pleased that he knew it too. "We're proud of you, Walter. I just got through talking with a man who is only a few years older than you are. He's going to have two bypasses tomorrow. He has a poor attitude, and I'm worried about how he will do after surgery because of it. I wish I could bring him down here to see you, but we have to keep him in the CCU because of continued heart pain."

"Walter," Julie said, "would you mind if I brought that man's family to see you?"

"Julie, anything I can do to make it easier for someone else, I'm more than happy to do."

"Thanks," Julie said. "If they can see how well you are doing just six hours after surgery, perhaps they can help John improve his attitude."

Mary and the children visited briefly with Walter and were surprised by his progress. Julie and I took them back to John's room. Then, after one last visit with Walter, we went to talk with Becky. The Waiting Room looked quite different from the smoky, tension-packed room we had seen earlier in the day. Becky and a close friend were the only people who remained. This morning there had not been an empty seat.

"Walter looks super, Becky." I sat down beside her. "As you know when you saw him at five thirty, we had the tube out of his windpipe. Since then, Julie and I stood him up beside the bed."

"You mean he has already been up?"

"He was glad to get off his back. I had to be kind of rough on him about his coughing, but I warned him about that before surgery. Everything else looks encouraging. We're getting ready to go home. After you see him at seven thirty you should go home and get some rest. You may think that all you did was sit around today, but emotional stress can be very fatiguing. It's like being in a car wreck—you don't notice the soreness until the next day. Tomorrow, you're going to be exhausted."

"I'm beginning to feel that way now," Becky said. "I thought I'd spend the night in the hospital, but if you promise to call tonight, I'd love to go home."

"I'll call between nine and ten," I said. "Remember, I'll call you at anytime if we have problems. But if you don't hear from me after the ten o'clock call, you can assume that Walter is okay."

Julie and I were tired, but it was a good kind of tired. The day had been a relatively short one for us, as compared to some. It was almost 7:00. We agreed to meet in the ICU at 5:45 the next morning.

If Walter had no significant problems in the next four to five hours, I knew that the chances of serious complications would be almost negligible. The sun was visible in the west, and I reassured myself that Walter undoubtedly would live to see another sunrise with Becky. But I was suddenly haunted by the question: Would Mary and John be as fortunate?

After dinner Sylvia and I went to sit on the porch outside of our bedroom.

"How does the man look for tomorrow?" she asked.

"He only needs two bypasses. This case should be considerably easier than the one we did this morning. But I'm concerned about his attitude. It stinks! First of all, he tried to deny that he even has heart disease, and second, he's not totally convinced he *needs* surgery. I wouldn't operate on him if I felt we could safely postpone surgery until his attitude improved."

"Can't you do anything to make it better?"

"Honey, we spent more pre-op time with John and his wife, Mary, who is really a sweet person, than we did with Walter and Becky. Walter had a heart attack seven or eight years ago, which convinced him he had heart disease. John still thinks his problem is indigestion rather than hardening of the arteries."

Later I called the ICU and the nurse reported that Walter was continuing to do well. She had gotten him up at nine, and he had done even better than when Julie and I had stood him earlier. This was usually the case, as most patients are still groggy that first time.

When I dialed Becky's number, the line was busy for at least ten minutes. Finally, I got through. "Becky, this is Tex. I guess your phone has been ringing all evening. This always happens. I bet you're amazed how many people heard about Walter's surgery and have called tonight."

I gave Becky the good report and said, "Things look good,

Becky. Don't forget, I expect you to be cheerful, just as I do Walter."

"You won't have to worry about that," Becky exclaimed. "The only person happier than I am is Walter!"

A short time later I crawled into bed and turned off the light. The darkness was restful to my eyes, but as soon as I tried to close them, I saw the pictures of John's arteriograms. The ritual of going over tomorrow's operation had begun. The challenge of Walter was behind me. Ahead lay possibly even greater challenges. After John, there was the woman who was almost seventy, and the man who would need his second open-heart operation.

Each of these cases would test my technical, physical, and emotional skills. The technical skills would be present as a result of my training and experience. The physical stamina would be replenished simply by sleep. But extra effort would be required to restore the emotional energy drained by each case.

The thrill of seeing Walter do well compensated partly for some of this drain. The realization that John meant just as much to Mary and their sons as Walter did to Becky and their two children would partially "recharge" me. Even so, there is an emotional drain with each case that is never totally replaced.

I gave thanks to Him for being with Becky and Walter today and asked that He be with Mary and John tomorrow. My prayer was cut short as pictures of the coronary arteriograms flashed through my mind. Some people count sheep, I count blocked heart arteries. I stopped the mental review of John's arteriograms long enough to say another prayer—that the phone would not ring tonight. If it should, it would set off a tremendous flow of adrenalin that would trigger wakefulness for at least another hour. My immediate reaction to any phone call tonight would be that something had gone wrong with Walter.

9

SYLVIA AND I had learned to awaken instinctively at about five each morning, a habit that had evolved from years of getting up at this time, beginning with my internship and residency. We awakened at five even on vacations. Setting a clock was a formality and done for insurance, in case our natural alarms failed to function. I called about Walter and learned that the night had gone well. Thirty minutes later I headed for St. John's, anxious to face what Tuesday would bring.

After parking, I hurried to John's room, wanting to spend some time with him before his "Whoopee Shot." I would make one last effort to improve his attitude pre-operatively.

John and Mary had been talking for almost an hour when I arrived. John seemed a little better. Possibly what Mary had said after seeing Walter the night before had helped. John knew the risks and seemed to accept them, but he still failed to show the fight and personal commitment to do well that I wanted him to have.

I asked John, "Do you have any questions? Are you ready to go?"

He said, "Yeah, Doc. I'm getting tired of lying in this bed. Anything would be better than this."

"Don't call me Doc." I nudged his bed. "Whether you like

it or not, you and I are going to get pretty close over the next week to ten days and I don't want you to call me Doc unless you want me to call you 'Patient.' I guess that means that Mary becomes 'Patient's Wife,' and I really don't want to call her that."

With a grin Mary replied, "No, Tex, I don't want you to call me that either. I think John just forgot."

John acknowledged sheepishly that he had. To me, this was only further evidence that I had failed to establish the bond that I feel is so important before surgery.

After visiting with John and Mary for a few minutes, I felt that nothing further could be done to improve John's mental outlook and left the CCU to see Walter. He was in excellent spirits, had been up four times during the night, and had grown stronger and more adept at getting in and out of the bed. Julie was with him and was busy removing the cannula from his wrist artery.

I had already checked Walter's chest X ray and reviewed the laboratory results that were taped to the front of his chart. After listening to his heart and lungs, as well as palpating his abdomen and checking for groin pulses, I said, "Your heart sounds good. Your lungs sound a lot better than they did last night. You obviously learned how to cough."

"I sure have tried. I don't want that tube put down my nose into my windpipe again!"

"Well, I can certainly tell the difference. Let's start getting these lines out and get you up walking. All you did last night was stand beside the bed. In a few minutes you're going to walk the length of the ICU."

I slowly removed the dressing from Walter's chest incision. He winced as the tape pulled on the skin that was now permanently engraved with the evidence that I had been there. I apologized for causing him discomfort, but reminded him to keep smiling.

While Julie continued to hold pressure on his wrist artery to keep it from bleeding, I took out the rest of the tubes. The i.v. line in the side of his neck was removed and a light pressure dressing was applied. I deflated the balloon that was retaining the catheter in Walter's bladder. Forewarning him that it would burn, I gently removed the soft rubber tube from his penis.

"Boy, that stings," Walter announced. "That thing has been miserable as hell. I thought I needed to pee all night. I kept asking the nurses for a urinal. In fact, I feel like I need to go right now."

"That's a normal sensation. Your bladder is in spasm from the irritation of the tube and its balloon."

Walter was now ready to walk. All lines and tubes, except for the chest tubes had been removed. Although there had been only a moderate amount of drainage during the night, I felt that there was still too much to remove the chest tubes at this point. I would probably remove them later this afternoon.

The nurse had given Walter two pain pills an hour earlier, anticipating the usual 'morning-after-surgery walk.' I have found that hypos are effective in relieving pain and discomfort after surgery, but they have the disadvantage of making the patient very sleepy. Certain pain pills give almost as much relief of pain, but patients remain alert and cooperative, sleeping only if they want to after taking them.

"If you're ready to go, let's get started," I said.

"I think I can get up on my own if you'll just let me pull on your arm," Walter said. His request surprised me, as I could not recall another patient who had been able to get out of bed on his own the first morning after surgery. I was even more pleased that the suggestion had come from Walter.

As we began our stroll through the ICU, Julie and I stayed close to Walter, one of us on each side. A nurse, carrying the container that collected the drainage from the chest tubes, joined our procession.

At first, Walter walked with a stiff right leg, guarding against the pain that resulted from the long incision extending from groin to ankle. The area across the knee joint caused him the most discomfort. Gradually the tightness in the knee area loosened and his gait became more natural. As we headed back toward his room from the far end of the ICU, his pace quickened. He walked with head high, proud of his performance.

"You're going great!" I said. "You have what I call 'the return-to-bed syndrome.' A patient tends to walk very slowly away from his room, but as soon as he turns around and realizes that he is heading back to bed, he walks faster."

Walter laughed. "Yeah, I know what you mean. I wasn't sure how far you were going to make me walk. As soon as I saw we were going back, I knew I had it made."

Walter was receptive to my suggestion that he sit up in a chair while the nurse finished making his bed. I placed a call to Becky from his room, knowing I would miss her at the 9:00 A.M. visiting hour—I would be in surgery. I told her that all the lines were out except the chest tubes, and that Walter had already walked the length of the ICU. Having reported this, I knew that there was nothing that would be more reassuring to Becky than hearing Walter's cheerful voice and handed the phone to him.

While they visited, I left the room to write orders and a progress note in Walter's chart. Then I gave him the plan for the day. "We're going to transfer you to Eight-West. I want you to walk in the halls—short to moderate distances, about what we walked this morning. You are to walk three or four more times today. I have one specific instruction, Walter: you're not to sit longer than twenty to thirty minutes at any one time for the next six weeks." I paused a moment to let this sink in. "You may walk or lie down, but you are not to sit for long periods of time. You can sit all day if you want, but every twenty to thirty minutes you must get up and walk around. When you sit for longer periods of time, because of gravity, blood begins to pool in your feet and the lower part of your body. When it pools, it tends to form clots. These clots can break off and go to your lungs. That's called a pulmonary embolus and can be life-threatening. There is no reason for you to die from something like this when it is preventable in most cases just by not sitting in one position for long periods of time.

"You must also work on your coughing. Your lungs sound pretty good now, but it is extremely important that you continue to cough every couple of hours. This keeps your lungs well expanded."

Satisfied that Walter understood, Julie and I left the ICU to begin rounds on the rest of our patients. She would see most of them with me, but at about 7:15 would leave to be with John in the Holding Room, as was her usual practice.

John's double vein bypass procedure went about as I expected. It didn't seem to go as smoothly as Walter's seven vessel bypass had. There were some problems getting John to come off the pump. Initially I thought this was because I had tried to come off the pump while his body temperature was still low. It then became obvious that this was not the problem. After going on and off the pump several times, and with the help of stimulating drugs, John's heart finally resumed adequate pumping function. He maintained a good blood pressure through the rest of the surgery, and no new problems developed. His electrocardiogram reverted to normal, which was the most encouraging sign.

The anxiety I experienced while getting John off the pump reminded me of my most difficult case, a young executive in his early forties who had suffered a massive heart attack. Jack had continued to have problems and had been readmitted to the hospital on several occasions because of what were thought to be small heart attacks. At first, after reviewing his cardiac cath, I had agreed with Jack's physicians that he was not a candidate for surgery because his heart was too severely damaged. After multiple readmissions, we all reconsidered Jack's case. We concurred that bypass surgery was the only thing that could offer him a chance of a reasonably normal life. Jack's attitude was superb, and I took him to surgery early one morning. Nine and a half hours later, after spending more than six hours on the heart-lung machine, we finally entered the ICU with a viable patient. Jack was requiring every kind of available artificial support to keep him alive.

Forty-eight hours later he was off all means of support, and he was home eight days post-op.

I have no doubt Jack survived because of his tremendous desire to live. Now, almost five years later, Jack continues to do very well. I see him at least once a month for he is not only my accountant, but he and his wife, Pam, are close personal friends. Every time I have a patient who has problems coming off the pump, I remember the challenge and ultimate success of Jack's case.

By early afternoon, John had been stable for several hours and was no longer requiring stimulating drugs. Julie and I had already brought Mary and the children in to see him. They were overjoyed that he had survived surgery. After answering several questions, Julie and I were ready for our next pre-op talk.

At sixty-eight, Grace looked much younger than her stated age. It was obvious that she and her husband, Charles, were very close. They enjoyed traveling together and were deeply involved with their grandchildren. Now, with her activities severely limited by angina, she was not content to be housebound for the rest of her life. She had been very receptive to the recommendation that she have bypass surgery.

The pre-op talk was well received. Julie and I were convinced that Grace and Charles were aware of and understood what lie ahead. We felt reasonably sure that they could handle any complications or problems that might arise. Charles was extremely supportive of Grace's decision to have the surgery. Their optimism was infectious.

Before leaving the hospital for the office, we checked on John. He was still under the influence of the anesthetic and had not progressed to the point where we could consider removing the tube from his windpipe. His post-op course still concerned me. Getting him through the surgery was only the first step. I wondered if there might have been some other way I could have approached John in his pre-op preparation, but Julie reminded me of all our other patients. We had prepared them in exactly the same way, and they had done very well after surgery. John had been one of the few patients who had gone to the OR with a lousy attitude. How well he would do post-op remained to be seen.

10

OUR OFFICE on Tuesdays is more like a family reunion than a gathering of patients in a physician's waiting room. On this afternoon we see patients for their post-op visit. It is an especially rewarding part of our practice, and we look forward to this follow-up care. Only a short time is spent in actual examination. Usually, the patients have seen their cardiologist or internist just before coming to see us. We listen to each patient's lungs and heart, and incisions are inspected and cared for. But most of the time is spent visiting with each patient and spouse and answering any questions that they might have. At the same time we establish new goals for them as they continue through various phases of recovery.

As with everything else we do, our office is run as informally as possible. Sylvia enjoys Tuesday afternoons as much as Julie and I do. She has the opportunity to meet the people who are not just patients, but have become friends. She hears so much from Julie and me about the patients and their families that she visualizes how each will look. It is amazing how often she is right.

While Julie and I are busy with one patient, Sylvia visits with those in the waiting room. She is always amused by their conversations. We've discovered that there is a spirit of competition among patients about the number of bypasses each has had. The patient with four bypasses may be disappointed to learn that another patient was the proud recipient of five or six. It is almost as if patients strive to hold the record for the greatest number of bypasses. They discuss their walks, vying with each other for the greatest distance. Another frequent topic is weight loss. Most patients realize its importance, and make an effort to do so. Considering that the majority of them had been heavy smokers who gave up cigarettes following surgery, the ability to lose weight is viewed with great pride and a sense of achievement.

Without a doubt, the most frequently asked question is, "How many times did Tex have to kick your bed?" This always results in a lively discussion and an effort to have the lowest score in this competition. Each Tuesday, new bed-kicking incidents are related. One teenager took the prize. He had been a very challenging patient. I had had to remind him repeatedly to be cheerful. One morning I failed to get the expected response and swiftly, but gently, bumped his bed. Much to my chagrin, he had a thermometer in his mouth which he almost bit in half out of sheer surprise as his bed was jolted. From that moment on he knew that he had to smile when anyone came into his room, even if it was half a smile because of a thermometer. He became an excellent patient, and never again did I have to issue a reminder.

On another occasion, a patient said, "Hell, I would have been *afraid* to die. I knew that Tex would have kicked my coffin."

Tuesday afternoon in the office was a time for hearty laughter, and, as a result, patients often had newly discovered incisional pain. Referred patients, being seen for the first time, frequently expressed surprise at the informality. They often felt left out of the conversation because they had no bypasses to brag about or bed-bumping stories to reveal.

On this particular Tuesday, after seeing most of the patients, Julie and I excused ourselves to go back to the hospital to check on John. Our patients understood that on the day of surgery, post-op patients come first. I will not jeopardize their care, and patients at the office are always pleasant and cooperative about the inevitable delays.

John's blood gases on flow-by oxygen were satisfactory, and we felt that the breathing tube could be removed. His vital signs had been stable since surgery, and once the tube was pulled he was able to express himself, much to his satisfaction. He had the usual discomfort of all open-heart patients, but was pleased that he had come through the surgery. After reassuring Mary about John's progress, we returned to the office to see the remaining patients.

It was after six before Sylvia, Julie, and I wrapped things up at the office. Julie and I embarked on the long process of evening rounds. On days when we had surgery, morning rounds were designed to uncover potential problems and trouble spots. Evening rounds, on the other hand, were made without a deadline to meet and we took as much time as each individual patient required. I had learned that problems dealt with and questions answered during the early post-op period prevented much unnecessary anxiety for the patient and family during the later phases of recovery.

John was having no significant problems, and his attitude was surprisingly good. Still, we stayed with him longer than we had with Walter at this stage, simply to help him maintain a positive outlook. We visited with Mary and, after completing rounds on the rest of the patients, arrived at Walter's room shortly before 8:00 P.M.

"Did you think we had forgotten you, Walter?" I asked. "I called to check on you a couple of times and got good reports."

"You just missed my fourth walk," Walter announced. "These darn tubes are really bothering me where they come out of my stomach. Otherwise I feel great."

I checked the level of the bloody fluid in the container that was hooked over the end of the bed and noted that there had been very little drainage in the last eight hours. Turning to Julie, I asked her to get the usual supplies for removal of the tubes.

"I'll bet that we can make you a lot more comfortable by getting these out," I said to Walter, and began to remove the dressings and sutures that secured his chest tubes.

"If the chest tubes go only into your heart sac cavity and not into the lung spaces, they can be removed slowly and gently. But if they go into your lung cavities as well as your heart sac, they need to be pulled rapidly. This prevents air from being sucked back through the tubes into the lung cavities and collapsing your lungs. Fortunately for you, the tubes are in the heart sac only and therefore can be pulled slowly. It is really important that you relax. These tubes go through your stomach muscles, and the worst thing you can do is tense up and tighten your muscles around them. That will make it hurt like hell. But if you relax, it won't be too bad. They'll be out in a few seconds."

Walter tried to relax his stomach muscles, but then tightened up. After again cautioning him to relax, I slowly removed the chest tubes. A small amount of bloody fluid ran down the side of his abdomen, and Julie blotted it with a gauze sponge. She then placed a small sterile dressing over the entrance wounds where the tubes had been.

"That wasn't as bad as you told me it was going to be," Walter said. "It feels better already."

Having him sit up, I was better able to examine his heart and listen to his lungs. There were no new significant findings on his physical exam.

"By listening to your lungs, I can tell that you have been

doing a pretty good job of coughing. But it's important that you continue to work at it. Let me hear you cough."

Walter had learned to hug a pillow against his chest as he coughed; the tighter he hugged the pillow, the more it splinted his sternal incision. Julie encouraged him to cough deeply so I wouldn't bring out the "snake," the catheter which I pass down the nose into the windpipe to stimulate coughing.

"I coughed better than this earlier today, but I don't seem to be able to get anything up," Walter said.

"It's not important that you bring something up every time," I said. "The important thing is that you cough. How much is brought up following surgery varies from patient to patient. Some need to cough up quite a bit of mucus, whereas others have very little. I'm surprised that you don't have more to bring up, since you're a heavy smoker. But your lungs sound fairly clear and your chest X-ray looks good, so you're probably okay. I still want you to cough, though. Your lungs are made up of millions of tiny balloons. You know how hard it is to blow up a very small balloon. You strain and strain to get it started; once you get it started it's easy to blow it up. The balloons in your lungs act the same way. Because it hurts to take a deep breath, the very little balloons in your lungs collapse and it takes a very strong, forceful cough to pop them open again. Once you open them up with a good cough, they will stay open. If they remain collapsed, bacteria collect in these areas and that's how you get pneumonia."

We showed Walter how to get back into bed on his own, teaching him to use his elbow to help lower himself to his side and then turn onto his back. Just after we had gotten him to bed, Becky appeared. She had gone to the coffee shop for supper, having waited all afternoon to see us.

"I just knew that if I left, that would be the time you would come. I so much wanted to talk with you."

"What's the matter, Becky?" I asked. "Walter is doing great. Is there something you're worried about?"

"Well, there are several things. One of them was the chest tubes. I see that they're already out. Also, Walter hasn't been eating much; he seems awfully tired, but hasn't been able to sleep."

"We leave the chest tubes in place until there is only minimal drainage. He had oozed very little this afternoon, so we felt we could remove them.

"He won't be very hungry. His appetite is poor and will be for the next four to six weeks. Pain pills dull the pain nerves, but they also dull all other nerves and sensations, including appetite. As long as he hurts, he will not be hungry, and as long as he continues to take pain pills, they will diminish his appetite. He will regain his strength by getting up and moving around, not by eating. Many families try to encourage patients to eat so that they will regain their strength. This just isn't the way it works. Patients regain their strength by exercising.

"Another thing," I turned to Walter and continued. "Because you don't have an appetite, your stomach gets used to not having much food in it. You will feel very hungry one of these days and Becky will go out of her way to cook your favorite meal. She will probably spend hours in the kitchen. You will sit down, take two bites, and then announce that you are full. Becky will be upset at your apparent lack of appreciation for her efforts. This will happen, so be prepared for it."

"Becky has been pushing me all day," Walter said, "trying to get me to eat and drink more. I just haven't felt like it. I'm glad she could hear this. She would have hounded me for weeks if you hadn't explained it."

"Now about the sleep," I said. "You didn't sleep at all last night because the nurses were constantly checking on you. You won't sleep much better tonight because you're still so uncomfortable. Only when you're two or three days out from surgery, will you finally get a good night's sleep.

"I need to warn you about a couple of things. Even though

you're not hungry, it's probably best to take your medications with crackers or small amounts of food and milk to prevent nausea. Some of the medications can be irritating to your stomach. It's important that you don't take them on an empty stomach unless it's a specific type of medication that's ordered that way. You should also be aware that any type of pain medication, whether it is a shot or pill, can be extremely constipating. You will need some help to prevent constipation, so I'll order a laxative for you. The nurses will be bringing in pills at various times during the day. These are ordered at specific times, but will not include pain pills, sleeping pills, or a laxative. You must ask for them specifically."

I paused. "By the way, Walter did you smile when Becky came through the door a few minutes ago? I'm not sure that I saw it." To emphasize my point I nudged his bed.

Walter immediately broke into a grin. "If I didn't, it was the first time I haven't."

Becky quickly came to his defense. "He's certainly been a much better patient this time than he was six years ago. For the first five to six weeks after his heart attack, he was a real bear."

I winked at Walter. "That's what comes from being threatened."

Our next stop was at Grace's room. I was much less concerned about her post-op course than I was about John's. I knew that if we got her through the surgery, she would do well, even if she was sixty-eight.

Sometimes I feel very close to a patient, and not as close to the rest of the family. At other times, I feel much closer to members of the family than to the patient. Of course, my greatest joy occurs when I feel equally close to patient and family. Such was the case with Grace and Charles. They were appreciative of everything the nurses and the aides did for her, and never complained. She was a true lady, and he a true gentleman. She would be a pleasure to care for after surgery.

The ICU was our last stop. It was 9:20 P.M. and I had almost forgotten to place the promised call to Mary. After helping John stand beside the bed, I called her and let her talk briefly with him.

It was almost 9:45 when I arrived home. After a bowl of cereal and a glass of instant breakfast, I was ready to drop. Sylvia knew it was fairly common for me not to be hungry. Often I was so tired that I only wanted to eat as quickly as possible, take a warm shower, and fall into bed.

I told Sylvia how surprised I was that my fears about John had not materialized, yet I knew that his situation had already taken its toll on me. After turning out the light, Grace's arteriograms flashed before me, and then exhaustion—more emotional than physical—cut her review course short. I would sleep more soundly on that Tuesday night than I had in the last four or five days.

11

ON WEDNESDAY morning, John was almost euphoric. He had had a reasonably good night, and had been up on four occasions. When he saw Julie and me, he responded with unexpected cheerfulness. We removed all the lines and tubes, except the chest tubes. We walked him the length of the ICU and were pleased with how well he did. I ordered him transferred to 8-West and called Mary with the good news.

Excessive optimism similar to John's is not unusual following open-heart surgery. Patients are so happy initially that they survived the surgery, they are oblivious to much of their pain. The real test of their spirit comes later.

After finishing with John, Julie and I went to the eighth floor and checked Walter's chart. We noticed he was running a low-grade fever. Slight temperature elevation is common for post-op open-hearts the first several days; the fever is usually a result of inflammation of the heart sac from surgery. But because of Walter's smoking habit, I needed to make sure that it wasn't due to early pneumonia. His weight was still seven pounds above what it had been pre-op. This excessive gain was due to the fluids pumped into him while he was on the heart-lung machine. I knew he would begin to pass most of this water through his kidneys over the next two to three days.

It was just dawn when we visited Walter. He had learned his lessons well and greeted us good-naturedly, but I noticed he hadn't shaved.

"How was your night, Walter?"

"Pretty good, Tex. I slept better than at any time since surgery, but I sure was sore this morning."

"I'm surprised you slept well last night," I said. "Most people don't get a good night's sleep until the third night after surgery. I always know when a patient gets his first good night's sleep. If he tells me he is sore all over, I know he slept well. The soreness comes from sleeping soundly and lying in one position for a long time. If you had not slept well and tossed and turned all night, you wouldn't be sore this morning."

"Well, I really *am* sore," Walter said. "I had to ask for two pain pills before I could get out of bed this morning. I've already walked in the hall, and got myself a cup of coffee."

I bumped the bed with my knee, just a little, but enough to startle him.

"What was that for?" He grimaced.

"That was for not being shaved the second morning after surgery. I thought that I had told you it would be okay if you didn't shave the day after surgery, but I expected you to be clean-shaven by this morning. If I didn't tell you, I meant to."

"Well, I would have if Becky hadn't taken my razor home and forgotten to bring it back."

"That excuse isn't good enough. You call her and ask her to bring it so that you are shaved by the time we make rounds this evening.

Patients do better if they are expected to be concerned about their appearance after surgery. I require the men to have their hair combed and be clean-shaven, the women to have their hair fixed and make-up on. The sooner they become concerned about their personal care, the better they do. Seeing the patient well groomed also makes a positive impression on the family.

I was pleased with how clear Walter's lungs sounded. I could still hear the faint rub with every heart beat.

"Let me hear you cough, Walter."

He responded with a fairly good effort, "I don't seem to be getting much up," he said, "but I'm still working at it."

"I want you to walk at least six times in the hall today. I'm not interested in having you walk long distances. In fact, I want you to walk six different times, rather than do six laps around the floor on one occasion, then be so exhausted that you can't get up again the rest of the day. The important thing is to be out of bed several times and rest between each walk. You should sit in a chair, too, but remember not to sit longer than twenty to thirty minutes at any one time."

Walter was very attentive throughout the discussion. This was in marked contrast to his behavior during the initial portion of his pre-op talk. It was very rewarding to Julie and me to see this change. As we prepared to leave, Walter said, "Tex, I have two questions. Why does my leg hurt, especially around the knee and in the groin area? And why do I have fluid draining from my leg incision?"

"Nearly every patient asks those same questions. The reason you have pain in your leg is not so much because of the length of the incision as it is from the tightness and placement of the stitches. Any time stitches cross a joint, or are in an area that moves a great deal, there is a lot more tension on the skin. This is what causes the tenderness and discomfort. Have you noticed that the lower part of your leg, near your ankle, is numb? The numbness results from me cutting the nerve that runs to the skin of that part of your ankle."

Walter nodded. He had noticed the increased redness around the stitches over the knee joint as well as in the groin area caused by the irritation from walking.

"The fluid that drains from your leg incision appears to be blood, but really isn't. Most of it is serum. When we opened your leg to take the vein, we burned, or cauterized, many of the small blood vessels. Just as you form a blister filled with serum when you burn your hand, so too, serum formed after we burned your blood vessels. When you walk, the pressure of your muscles forces this serum and a small amount of blood that is free under the skin out through the incision. It is not a sign of infection and is not really anything you need to worry about. It will probably continue for another week or ten days."

Because of her age, Grace had not received as strong a "Whoopee Shot" as Walter or John did. She was therefore much more alert than they had been. She greeted me cordially and smiled when I entered OR 16. Julie was at her side. After anesthesia had been safely induced and all the tubes and lines were in, Julie and I placed the first call to Charles.

Some cardiovascular surgeons have suggested that women, especially those over the age of sixty, do not seem to do as well with coronary artery bypass surgery as men do. I have not found this to be true. In fact, I would much rather operate on a woman with an excellent attitude, regardless of her age, than operate on someone with a poor attitude.

Grace's operation was more difficult than expected because her vein was very thin-walled. We went on the pump without significant problems, but the time her heart was without blood supply was prolonged because of technical difficulties associated with the vein. Trying to suture a thin vein to a thin-walled coronary artery is much like sewing butter to butter. And that's butter that has been sitting out of a refrigerator for twelve hours in a hot kitchen!

She came off the pump sluggishly at first, but gradually her heart function improved. The rest of the operation went smoothly. Once Grace was settled in the ICU, we brought Charles in to see her. She was still under the anesthetic and did not respond to him, which I assured him was not unusual. Many patients, especially the older ones, take longer to wake up after anesthesia.

Julie and I stayed with Grace in the ICU longer than usual. I was concerned over the amount of oozing, and I wanted to be sure that she hadn't suffered a stroke. Finally, satisfied that she was going to be okay, we left the ICU to talk with Charles about her status.

By late Wednesday afternoon, Grace had become fully conscious and no longer required the breathing machine. Her blood gases on flow-by oxygen were excellent, attributed to the fact that she had never smoked. Now, a few hours after surgery, she was ready to have the tube removed from her windpipe.

It is most unusual for me to perform vascular surgery on a patient who has never smoked cigarettes. Grace was one of those rare individuals. However, she had a strong family history of heart disease. Her parents had died in their mid-sixties of heart attack. One brother and a sister also had died of heart attack. Her only living brother was fifty-seven and was having angina. Because he was a smoker, he had developed problems at a younger age than she. He had recently experienced a light heart attack, which prevented him from being with Grace during her surgery.

We pulled the tube out of Grace's windpipe. Her blood pressure and pulse were stable. She had oozed a moderate amount of blood since surgery, but this blood loss had been replaced with transfusions and we felt we could safely get her up. She was hesitant when I first mentioned that we were going to stand her, but after she realized that I was serious, she complied and was gotten up without difficulty. After having her cough and walk in place, we helped her back to bed.

"Grace, you did great this morning. We brought Charles in to see you earlier, but you weren't awake yet. Now, it's very important that you work on your coughing. Even though you never smoked, you can still get pneumonia if you don't clear the mucus out of your windpipe. I know it hurts, but you have to cough."

"It doesn't hurt that much. And even if it does, I'll do it."

I had no doubt that Grace would continue to do exceptionally well. She was one of those extraordinary patients who could rise above her own physical pain and discomfort. As my own personal way of saying "Thanks, Grace, for doing so well," I leaned over and kissed her.

"I'm amazed," Charles said later, "that someone who is almost seventy can go through this type of surgery and be up this soon."

"Age is not a deterrent to major surgery," I said. "Patients with a superb attitude like Grace has will do well no matter how old they are."

12

ON WEDNESDAY, outside the ICU, Julie and I came upon a woman alone and weeping. Her husband, we discovered, had undergone extensive surgery this morning.

"I'm not exactly sure what they did," she said between sobs, "but it took a long time. When it was over, the doctor called and said that my husband was all right and that I could see him when the nurses said it was okay. I stayed in the Waiting Room, but nobody came to get me. I didn't know about the regular visiting period at 1:00 P.M. Finally, I came here, and they said I could see him. He looked horrible. The doctor had said he was doing fine, but it was hard to believe, what with all those tubes and things in him. He looked as if he were dying."

Julie and I exchanged a knowing glance. We had been through this experience on other occasions. I tried to console the woman. "If your husband's doctor said he was all right, then he is. Those tubes are to give him the best care possible. If you can tell me what you're upset about, I will try to explain as much as I can to you."

After listening to her, I said, "The large tube in his mouth goes into his windpipe. It is connected to a breathing machine. He can't talk to you because the tube goes between his vocal cords. The smaller tube, in his nose, goes down into his stomach. It will help prevent his stomach from becoming distended. There are several reasons why he is so pale. First, he is very cold because of the cool environment of the OR. Blood vessels close down or constrict when exposed to cold, causing the skin to blanch. He probably was also given a lot of i.v. fluids during the operation. The fluids dilute his blood, which in turn washes out his color, adding further to his pallor. He will look much better when his temperature gets back to normal, the tube is removed from his windpipe, and he can talk to you. It may be several days before they remove the tube that goes to his stomach. Only then will he begin to look as he did before surgery."

Her reply was valid. "I wish someone had told me what to expect. When I saw my husband, that was the biggest shock of my life. I was sure something had happened to him and I hadn't been told." She wiped her eyes and gently blew her nose.

In my opinion no physician ever does this to a patient's family on purpose. Many times we are accused of putting a family through such an unfortunate episode because we didn't want to take the time. We are seen as being too busy. In reality this is probably rarely the case. I believe that there are other explanations.

First, we see patients immediately post-op in the ICU on a daily basis. In effect, we develop an immunity to their swollen faces, pallor, and the multiple tubes and lines. To us, these people look like the patients we admitted to the ICU from surgery yesterday and the day before that. They all look much the same. They are alive, and that's what counts. But we fail to remember that patients who may look "normal" to us look ghastly to their families. A brief pre-op explanation by physicians or nurses to the patient and family would alleviate this problem. There should be a description of what the patient will look like and an explanation for each tube. And it would be ideal if the nurse taking care of a critically ill patient would make it a practice to intercept the family before family members see their loved one for the first time after admission to an Intensive Care Unit.

A second possible reason for apparent neglect of patients and their families is more difficult to put into words. Soldiers who lose their buddies on the battlefield are reluctant to make new friends among the replacements. It is easier to face the fear of battle and death alone than to go through the loss of another buddy.

Physicians and nurses experience a similar phenomen. Every patient is capable of hurting us—by dying. In an effort to shield ourselves from this emotionally trying experience we tend to avoid close personal relationships with patients and families. Nurses often stand mute at the bedside or leave the room as a family approaches—rarely introducing themselves for fear of becoming "involved." Some physicians keep their distance by talking to families by phone rather than facing them in a Waiting Room. These are examples of what might be called emotional self-preservation.

Physicians and nurses have been criticized for being "cold" and impersonal. But those who criticize probably have never had to face a family and deliver the message that a loved one has died. For a physician, this is compounded by the burden of feeling personally responsible for the patient's death. If you don't believe me, put yourself in a surgeon's position and take a patient who cheerfully kisses his family good-by as he enters the OR, then five hours later, face this same family with the news "he didn't make it."

I have never gotten used to telling a family that a loved one has died, and I don't believe that this ever becomes easy for any physician. In order to make such a situation more tolerable, we often keep our distance. To have to carry news of death to a family with whom you are only casually acquainted is difficult. To give the same message to people who have become close friends can be devastating. And so we avoid getting close to those who have the power to hurt us deeply.

I am not trying to protect physicians or to make excuses for them. I am only pointing out some of the factors that might contribute to unfortunate episodes such as the one witnessed outside the ICU. Nearly every physician I have worked with has been excellent in his or her particular specialty. Most have had superb training. There is little variation in the way physicians from different residency programs handle patients with the same illness. The real difference lies in how each physician responds to the emotional and supportive needs of the patients and their families. I believe that the extent to which physicians become emotionally involved is directly proportional to their willingness to risk being hurt.

Much has been written about why people go into medicine. Such factors as prestige, financial security, and independence certainly play a role. But I believe that the reason that surpasses all others is a basic desire to be of service to our fellow human beings.

I suspect that there are also some underlying psychological needs that are met when a person chooses medicine as a career. We harbor either a profound fear of death or a definite fear of pain. We enter medicine in order to be in a position to control, and to have an understanding of, those situations that give rise to these fears.

Those of us who have a fear of death project this fear to our patients. The death of any patient is threatening to us, and we will do anything we can to protect against this threat. Some of us shield ourselves emotionally by placing barriers between us and our patients. We resist all forms of closeness in order to minimize the psychological effects of their death. Others may do everything possible to prolong life, irrespective of its quality, in order not to have to confront death. Prolonged use of heroic and extraordinary efforts to keep someone "alive" in the presence of "brain death" exemplifies such an approach. The ability to control, to a certain extent, not only the living but also the dying of a patient gives us a feeling of security. When a patient dies, our feeling of security is badly damaged. His or her death makes us realize that someone greater than ourselves is in absolute control. We are shocked back to the reality of our own vulnerability to death.

There are those of us who do not fear death, but rather have a deep-seated fear of pain. For us, death would be a welcome relief were we suffering from the relentless pain of terminal cancer. We project this fear to our patients, doing everything we can to alleviate their physical discomfort with narcotics or analgesics. In cases where there is no hope of survival, we are willing to stop heroic measures that might prolong the suffering.

During Christmas vacation in my first year in medical school, I made hospital rounds with my father, who is also a physician. One of his elderly patients was dying of cancer. In constant pain, she required increasing amounts of narcotics. She was heavily sedated and nonresponsive. Upon development of pneumonia, discussion between my father and the family resulted in a joint decision to stop treatment, but he promised to keep her as comfortable as possible. I was appalled that my father, a physician dedicated to saving lives, was not going to do everything he could to keep this woman alive. Later, we had a lengthy discussion. I shall never forget what he said: "I believe in doing everything possible to prolong the living; I do not believe in prolonging the dying." He cautioned me that this philosophy might be difficult to accept, but if I ever did accept it, I would live by it. I did, and I have!

My father's decision to refrain from "prolonging the dying" taught me an even greater lesson. Not only was he protecting the patient from intense pain by letting her die, he was also bringing relief to her family by not prolonging the nightmare of watching her suffer.

Physicians are not alone in the fear of death or the fear of pain; they just have to face it daily and cope with it. I believe that everyone has one or the other of these two innate fears. Frequently, patients express to me their fear of death. They threaten me if I don't get them through surgery. They may pretend to joke, but they wouldn't have said it if they didn't mean it. "My children will haunt you forever if you don't get me through the surgery" is a common example of such threats.

Then there are those patients who fear physical pain and question me at length about how much discomfort they are going to have. They repeatedly ask me to promise complete relief of their post-op pain. The more unselfish patients are much less concerned about their own physical pain than they are about the emotional suffering that their families will have to endure. "Promise me that you won't keep me alive on machines" or "Don't let my family come in to see me until all of those tubes are out" are examples of statements I frequently hear. These patients often preface such statements with "I'm not afraid to die; just don't make my family suffer."

Wilfred Grenfell once said, "Life is either an arena of competition where one seeks to battle to the top at the expense of one's fellow man or life is a field of honor where one gives of oneself in service to one's fellow man." I feel that all people, but most especially those of us in this "field of honor" including physicians, nurses, clergy, etc., are not doing all we can. We must do more to help people face the possibilities of pain or the uncertainties of death. We must become more oriented toward preventing the emotional trauma of families facing the illness of a loved one.

Patients also have an obligation to adopt a similar attitude of concern for their families. A patient's cheerful attitude in the presence of pain and illness can do more than anything else to alleviate the emotional distress of concerned loved ones. My primary purpose for making a patient smile under the threat of having his bed kicked is not to make him smile for me. It is solely to insure that he is considerate of, and reassuring to, his family. This same cheerfulness extended by patients to physicians, nurses, aides, and clergy almost always evokes a response of warmth and genuine concern. Caring for a pleasant patient is always a privilege for me.

Physicians are accustomed to suffering and sickness, almost to the point of becoming unaffected. But the very environment in which we feel comfortable can seem hostile to others. For the average person, merely entering a hospital to visit a sick friend can be upsetting. To be a patient awaiting surgery or the results of diagnostic tests can be frightening. And the seemingly interminable wait outside surgery or an Intensive Care Unit for news of a critically ill loved one can be a terrifying experience, for people often fear the worst.

As physicians, all of us have to become more attentive to the psychological needs of the patients, but we must also make even greater efforts to become more closely involved with the families. When one of our own family members becomes ill, we use every means possible to keep abreast of the patient's progress. We review the chart, call the attending physician, or exercise our authority in any other way necessary to remain informed. We do this because we cannot tolerate the emotional suffering of not knowing.

The families of our patients deserve this same treatment. We must treat families with the same courtesies that we expect when we sit in a Waiting Room while our loved ones undergo surgery or while they lie critically ill in an Intensive Care Unit. We have to be willing to get close to patients and their families despite the risk of emotional trauma to ourselves when we lose a patient who has become a friend. I have found, through personal experience, that herein lies the real challenge and the immeasurable joy of the practice of medicine.

13

I DON'T HAVE to smile all the time," John said in a bitchy tone.

Obviously, his initial euphoria was over. This was the attitude I feared he would have. Responding as I had promised I would, I bumped his bed with my thigh. No one in the room, including John, doubted that I meant it.

"I told you that you were not going to use this operation, or the pain associated with it, to upset your family or to get sympathy," I said. I really don't care what you think of *me*. I have one job to do, and that's to get you well and out of this hospital alive. But I will not tolerate you being bitchy to the nurses or to your wife. Do you understand?"

John clutched the sides of the bed to ward off another bump. "What if I don't feel like smiling?" he said angrily. "I'm in pain. Why do I have to smile?"

"John, I know that you have pain, but that doesn't make any difference."

I pulled up his hospital gown to examine him. The usual rub between the heart and its sac was present, but I was much more concerned about the absence of good breath sounds in the lower half of both lungs. This was an early sign of pneumonia, and was possibly contributing to his present fever.

"Your lungs sound terrible. You haven't been coughing worth a damn. The nurses also told me that you wouldn't walk in the hall earlier. How come?"

John continued to display belligerence. He was upset that he had come to the hospital in the first place. He was angry that he had needed surgery, and was hostile toward me and everyone else involved with his care. The fact that the nurses had "ratted" on him certainly didn't help matters. "I didn't feel like getting up," he countered.

"I don't give a damn how you feel!" I bumped the bed again, this time a little harder. "You're going to do exactly what the nurses tell you to do. Don't get upset with them, they're only carrying out my orders. If you want to get mad at somebody, get mad at me."

John was now almost exploding with anger, but he realized that I held all the aces. Finally he began to give in, and a forced, weak grin appeared. "Okay, Doc." he said.

I took a step backward, placed my right foot on the end of his bed and threatened to kick it across the room. "Don't call me that. You don't learn your lessons very well, do you, Mr. Patient? I gave you two rules before surgery. First, you have to call me Tex. Second, you have to smile when any of us come in the room. Those two rules still apply. Is that clear, Mr. Patient?"

"Okay, Tex." He held both hands up with palms extended. His smile was no longer forced. For the first time since I had met him, he seemed to understand my message.

I sat down on the bed and gestured for Mary to sit in the chair beside us. "John, seriously, there is a reason for everything we do. We get you up so early after surgery to prevent complications. Patients who stay in bed get pneumonia. If you lie in bed in one position for prolonged periods of time, you run the risk of developing blood clots in your legs. We also want to prove to you that you aren't going to fall apart. It is just as safe to get you up four hours after surgery as it is to get you up four days after surgery. And finally, the longer you lie in bed, the longer it takes to re- cuperate following surgery. The sooner you're up, the better you will do and the faster you will regain your strength."

Lowering my voice, I continued. "Your lungs sound terrible; you haven't been coughing and haven't been getting up. When you're lying in bed, your intestines and stomach push up on your lungs and decrease the space that they can fill. But when you're up, gravity pulls the intestines down in the pelvis, allowing your lungs to expand more fully. Walking makes you take longer and deeper breaths. You also cough much better when you are sitting or standing."

"I know you're doing everything for a reason, Tex. It's all for my benefit. I'll try to do better."

"You'll not only try, you *will* do better! Julie and I will see to that. One other thing. You have the head of your bed elevated too high. So far as I'm concerned, this is a sitting position. Re- member, you may walk or lie down, but you're not to sit longer than twenty to thirty minutes, whether in a chair or in bed."

John pressed the button to move the head of his bed from upright to a much flatter position. "Is this okay?"

"That's a lot better. Now sit up so we can work on your coughing."

John's effort to cough was dismal, and I was forced to resort to the "snake." I listened to his lungs again and was satisfied with the improvement.

After removing his chest tubes, we walked him the length of the hallway. "See, you can walk as well as I can. If the nurses even hint that you should walk, do exactly as they say."

John smiled. "Okay. I know they're trying to help me."

Walter threw back the sheets and sat up on the side of the bed to show us how well he was doing.

"There's such a difference between you and the man we just saw," I said. "His attitude is as bad as yours is good." I sat down on the bed. "Are you having any problems, Walter?"

"I have pain, mainly in the shoulders and chest." He rubbed each shoulder and pointed to his ribs. The painful points over his ribs were several inches to either side of his sternal incision.

"Every one of my patients complains of soreness in the same places." I shook my head dejectedly. "I guess I should go back to school and learn how to do this operation right. Seriously, let me explain that pain. Your collarbone is attached to your shoulder. When we divide the breastbone and spread it apart nine or ten inches, tremendous pressure is put on your shoulders by the collarbone. The reason your ribs are more tender than your incision is that your ribs come around to the front and stop several inches from the breastbone. The rest is cartilage. When the breastbone is spread apart, it puts pressure on this junction between the ribs and cartilage, which often breaks or fractures. Fractured cartilage is much more painful than a broken rib and also takes much longer to heal. You will be sore in those areas for another eight to ten weeks. There's nothing to do but get used to it."

"Just so I know that the pain isn't my heart."

"Walter, this pain isn't the same type of pain you had when you had your heart attack, is it?"

"No, when I had my heart attack I felt as though someone was sitting on my chest or a vise was squeezing me. It went into my jaws and down both arms. It was much different from this pain."

"Then you don't have to worry. Heart pain will always be the same. Pain that isn't exactly like your heart-attack pain is incisional pain that I have caused, not angina. You only have to worry if you begin to have that pressure-type pain that you had with your heart attack, or the angina that you had a couple of weeks ago. Any other type of pain, you can blame on me."

Becky asked, "Is it normal for him to have a bad sore throat and be hoarse?"

"All patients have a sore throat the first few days after surgery, Becky. The tube that was in Walter's windpipe caused it. Many patients are also hoarse because the tube went between the vocal cords. Every time they took a breath, the tube moved up and down causing blisters to form on the vocal cords. These small blisters keep the vocal cords from coming together completely and the result is hoarseness. Trying to talk while the tube is in place can make the blisters even worse. It may take weeks for his voice to return to normal."

"Well, I'm relieved that his sore throat isn't due to an infection. He's been so quiet this afternoon, and I was afraid something was wrong." Becky sighed.

"I think Walter is going through the usual post-op blues. We see this in almost every patient. The best comparison I can make is with post-partum blues. Remember how excited you were those first days after having a baby? You were so glad you had a normal child. You could wear clothes that looked nice on you, and Walter would want to make love to you again. Those first two or three days were wonderful. Then about the fourth or fifth day home, while feeding the baby at two in the morning, it suddenly struck you. Here I am, up with the baby and Walter is asleep. What if he leaves me and I have to feed and clothe this child and get him through school on my own! Suddenly things didn't look so great after all."

I turned to Walter, "The same thing is true about your surgery. The first two or three days after surgery most patients, like you, are euphoric because they didn't die, have a massive hemorrhage, or suffer a stroke. You are on cloud nine. Then, about the fourth or fifth day, you go through the post-op blues. Becky isn't checking on you every minute. She doesn't seem nearly as concerned as she did the first couple of days. Julie and I aren't in to see you as frequently. Neither are the nurses. All of a sudden it dawns on you that the people who were giving you sympathy and encouragement are now paying attention to others. You begin to feel sorry for yourself and wonder why you're not progressing as well as you were a couple of days earlier. This is a normal response. I usually don't let patients go home until I'm sure they have gone through this stage."

Walter had listened intently. He smiled and nodded. "I'm not sure that I've got it that bad, but I know what you're talking about. That's exactly the way I felt this afternoon. Now that I know it is normal, I don't think it will bother me as much."

"If you started having the depressed feeling this afternoon, you are going through it a lot sooner than most people. Many don't have it until the fourth to the seventh day."

After examining Walter, I asked, "How many times have you walked today?"

"At least six times and I plan to go once or twice more later this evening."

"Well, let's see how well you do."

Julie helped him put his robe on, and I helped him with his slippers. We started down the hall. Walter was walking faster than I was.

Becky looked up as we came back, striding briskly through the doorway. "I don't need to tell you how well he's doing," I said. "You can see that for yourself."

Walter had one final question before we left. "Can you give me something for my smoking? I want to smoke so badly I'd eat a cigarette if I had one."

"I'll be glad to give you something for your nerves to help you stop smoking. But there's no medication I can give you that will prevent you from smoking. *You* have to make a total commitment never to smoke again. It's completely up to you."

I sat down in a chair next to Walter. What I had to say was

very important for his future health. I didn't want to appear impatient or in a hurry.

"Walter, smoking accelerates the process of hardening of the arteries faster than any other factor. There's no question in my mind that your heart attack at such a young age was a result of cigarettes. Look how fast your blockages progressed over the past six years. You had a cath just after your heart attack and it wasn't felt that you needed bypass surgery at that time. Now, six years later, because of your continued heavy smoking, you've developed blockages severe enough to require seven bypasses. If you want to make sure you'll need this operation again, keep on smoking. I can guarantee you that if you smoke, you will. Some patients who smoke heavily after their bypass surgery develop new blockages either in their own coronary arteries or in their bypass grafts within six months. Out of one hundred open-heart patients I operate upon, approximately ninety-five of them are cigarette smokers. We did operate on a woman this morning who was not a smoker. But she was almost seventy before she developed heart problems. If she had smoked, she would have developed problems at a much younger age. She inherited her coronary artery disease from her parents, both of whom died from heart attack. But if you want to smoke, go ahead."

I gently poked at his chest incision, and Walter brought his hands up to protect himself. "What was that for?" he asked.

"I just want to remind you how much this hurts," I said. "You had to undergo this surgery because of smoking, and I want you to be sure to thank all those cigarettes for the pain you're having. I also want to remind you how painful this surgery is and make you realize that you'll go through the same pain if you have this operation again. If you smoke I can promise you that you'll need it."

I turned to Julie. "Why don't you call surgery and put him on the schedule for about six months from now?"

Walter laughed. "I get the message. I just thought I wanted to have a cigarette. Don't worry, I don't want to have to go through this again. I promise you, I won't smoke."

Knowing that we had made an impression on both Becky and Walter, Julie and I left. We still had to talk with the patient scheduled for surgery in the morning.

14

THE PRE-OP talk had been scheduled for 5:30. When we realized that we were going to be late, Julie had called to tell Dick and Jackie that it would be closer to 6:30.

Dick, who had recently moved his family to town, had undergone open-heart surgery in another city at the age of forty-nine. He had always smoked heavily and had continued to do so since his surgery. He was a perfect example of what I had just discussed with Walter.

As we came into Dick's room, they looked apprehensive. "I'm sorry we're late," I said. "We were taking care of post-op patients. They come first. Tomorrow is your day, and I promise I'll stay with you as long as you need me."

Julie and I introduced ourselves to Dick and Jackie's three children. After all were comfortably seated, I began my usual pre-op talk. While discussing Dick's alternatives, one of the children asked, "Why have these new blockages developed so quickly? I thought the first operation bypassed all the blockages."

"This was true when they did it eight years ago. Since then, your dad continued to smoke and he's developed blockages in his vein bypass grafts. What's more, there's a new blockage in one other heart artery. So we'll have to bypass both of the arteries that were operated on before, as well as the newly blocked artery, for a total of three bypass grafts."

"You mean that because I smoked, I developed blockages in the vein grafts?" Dick asked with surprise.

"I can't be positive that's the reason. But I *can* say that most of the people I have had to reoperate on following vein bypass surgery were those who continued to smoke. There are other things that can cause blockages in the grafts, but in my experience smoking is the most frequent reason."

"I wish someone had told me that. Maybe I would have quit."

"Now, Dick. I'm sure your doctors warned you repeatedly that smoking was not good for you. They may not have told you specifically that it would cause blockages in the grafts, but I know that most doctors are aware of this problem. You probably thought that because it took you forty-nine years to develop blockages in your heart arteries, you would have another forty-nine years before the new vein grafts would develop blockages. By that time, you would be ninety-eight. Who wants to live that long anyway? But it doesn't work that way. You can develop new blockages in the vein bypass grafts, or new blockages in your own arteries on downstream from where the grafts were placed, within a year or less if you persist in smoking."

After going over the usual risks—death, heart attack, stroke, hemorrhage, pneumonia, and infection—I added, "There's one additional risk that makes your surgery different. The fact that you have been operated on before increases your chance of dying during the operation from about four percent to around ten percent. You probably recall that right after your first surgery you were much more aware of your heart beat."

Dick nodded.

"During your first open-heart surgery, your breastbone was spread and the heart sac exposed. This sac was opened and the fluid surrounding your heart was removed. This fluid had acted as a shock absorber, much the same way water in a swimming pool absorbs the shock of someone diving into the water several feet away from you.

"Many surgeons do not close the heart sac at the completion of surgery. I usually don't, because the closed sac may kink the bypass grafts. In checking the report of your previous surgery, I found that yours had not been closed. As a result, your heart is probably right up against the back of your breastbone. This is why you experienced a significant thumping sensation against your sternum right after surgery. Almost every patient has this sensation."

"I know what you're talking about, Tex. Those first couple of months I thought the whole bed was shaking when I lay in certain positions."

"This not only explains the thumping sensation you had, but also why there is an added risk in your case. It may take a couple of hours longer for your operation this time, simply because we have to be so careful in getting through the breastbone. When we open the sternum, we may find that your heart has grown to the back side of it. You can see that if I divide the breastbone and cut into your heart at the same time, the only way that I can stop the bleeding is to expose the heart by spreading the breastbone. If I spread it, and the heart is stuck to it, I will spread the heart wide open. You will bleed to death, and the operation will be over within seconds. This rarely happens, but if it does, it is usually fatal."

I paused to let the significance of this sink in.

"Once we are through the breastbone, I'll begin to dissect the heart away from its sac. The fluid that used to be in the heart sac has been replaced by scar tissue. It will probably take us an hour or so just to dissect the scar tissue away from the heart. Only then can we finally begin to put you on the heart-lung machine and perform the rest of the operation."

I turned to Jackie and the rest of the family. "I will do everything I can to make tomorrow as easy as possible for you. You can see from the discussion so far that I will be honest with you. There will be multiple calls from surgery. A nurse will call to let you know when we are through the breastbone. I'll have her call again when we have the heart dissected free. If we have a problem with hemorrhage, we'll call to let you know. Once we get through the breastbone and are on the pump, the risk of surgery drops significantly."

"I'm glad you're going to make those calls," Jackie said. "It was horrible eight years ago. We waited and waited and never heard anything from surgery. I don't think I could go through that again." She closed her eyes, as if she were reliving a bad dream.

In the remainder of the pre-op talk, I gave Jackie the projected time schedule, and told her when she could expect the other calls from surgery, including when we got Dick on the pump, were halfway through the bypass procedure, were off the pump, and were starting to close. Then I presented my usual rules for smiling and calling me Tex.

Julie and I felt good about the pre-op talk. Dick and Jackie were warm and receptive. In a short time, a close relationship had developed among the four of us. It was going to be a pleasure taking care of Dick and his entire family. Before leaving St. John's, Julie and I checked on Grace.

"I've already been up a second time. I did better than the first time," she said with pride.

It was a little after eight when I got home. Gary was excited about his performance at today's soccer practice, and Monte was looking forward to his football scrimmage Friday night. He wanted Sylvia and me to come, and I promised him we would try to make it.

I love football and was anxious for the new season to start. In high school I had played quarterback, but my career was cut short by the first of two knee surgeries. My first operation was the day after Thanksgiving, 1959, and the second was the day after Thanksgiving, 1969. Each year around Thanksgiving I step very cautiously. On Thanksgiving, 1979, I stayed in bed!

My knee surgeries taught me a great deal about being a patient and about handling pain. There was no pre-op talk to prepare me for the pain I would experience with the first surgery. When I came out of the anesthetic, I hurt so bad I thought my leg had been amputated. I was in bed five days before I could develop enough strength to even raise the cast off the bed. I required frequent hypos. I was a terrible patient.

The second knee operation came during my internship year. Again I received no pre-op instruction, but because of my previous experience I knew exactly what to expect. Psychologically and emotionally I prepared myself for the pain and set my own post-op goals. Following this operation, I was up on crutches the afternoon of surgery and required few medications during my recovery. I was home in three days. This experience taught me how important being prepared for pain and discomfort can be. When unprepared patients awaken with pain after surgery, it does very little good to try to convince them that they should have "expected" it to hurt.

Sylvia and I went to bed early; I was exhausted. Dick's case would probably be the most difficult one I would do all week. I visualized his coronary arteries. I was confident that I could easily find two of the arteries because the previous bypass grafts would lead me right to them. The third artery would be much harder to find, as was always the case in a re-do operation. Arteries are difficult to find on a normal heart, but much more difficult to locate when there is a lot of scar tissue. Even so, I was not nearly as concerned about finding the arteries as I was about getting through the breastbone. That was only the first step, and once we were through the sternum, we still faced long periods of slow, tedious dissection. Each time I drifted off to sleep, I awakened in a cold, clammy sweat, startled by the sudden appearance of gushing blood as I tried in vain to dissect Dick's heart from the scar tissue that surrounded it.

15

GRACE had an excellent night. She had been up four times, getting stronger each time. I bent over and kissed her on the forehead. "You're a real doll, Grace. If you were doing any better, I'd have to send you home."

"I feel well enough to go home."

"Well, you're not quite ready for that yet. Maybe in a couple of days. You oozed a little more than usual after surgery. Have you been taking aspirin at home?"

"Yes, I take two almost every morning for my arthritis. It really helps my hands and shoulders."

"That's probably the reason you oozed so much after surgery. All forms of aspirin act as weak blood thinners. They work on the platelets in your blood, interfering with their ability to form clots. This is beneficial, but it can cause some minor bleeding problems in surgery. It made it a little harder to stop the bleeding, but it wasn't a big problem."

Knowing that Grace would need more transfusions, I explained this to her. "Your blood count is a little lower than I like to see. It's your only abnormal lab value this morning. The count is down because of the bleeding after surgery, and also because of the heart-lung machine. When your blood and platelets go through the heart-lung machine, many are injured or destroyed.

Once injured, they are removed from circulation by your own body mechanisms. Therefore, your blood count will slowly drift lower over the next couple of days. We're going to give you two blood transfusions today, and we may need to give you several more later in the week, so don't be alarmed when they come in to hang the blood. It's not because you are hemorrhaging. Be sure to explain this to Charles and tell him that it is not uncommon. In fact, it's unusual *not* to need transfusions following heart surgery."

During our walk around the ICU, the only tenderness Grace mentioned was the leg incision. Otherwise, she had few complaints and was unbelievably cheerful. I told her that she would be transferred to the eighth floor and cautioned her about sitting for long periods of time. She would be expected to walk in the halls at least three or four more times today, with the help of the nurses because she still had her chest tubes.

Julie and I continued rounds. We had stopped by to see Dick and Jackie before visiting Grace. Since many of our patients had been discharged, we would be able to spend more time with Walter and John. We were surprised to see that Mary was already with John.

"Hi, Doc." John quickly corrected himself, "I mean, Tex."

"Hi, John. How was your night?"

"Just fair. I was awake most of the time, tossing and turning. I never could get comfortable."

"That's pretty normal the first couple of nights after surgery. Usually patients are so sore they just can't sleep. After the third day, the worst pain begins to let up and you can expect to get more sleep. How are you doing otherwise?"

"All right, I guess. I hurt like hell."

"Have you been up walking this morning?" This was a baited question. I could see the half-full urinal on his bedside table.

"Hell, I'm so sore I haven't even tried to get out of bed!"

"You still haven't learned your lesson, have you? I told you to smile, even when you're complaining about pain." I bumped his bed. "Now get your tail out of bed and get going. I don't want you to use that urinal anymore. Go to the bathroom like a normal person; you're not an invalid. The more you get up and move about, the less soreness you'll have. I see that you haven't shaved. You are to shower and shave. By the time I see you this afternoon I want you to be cleaned up."

Turning to Mary, I asked, "What are you doing here so early?"

"John called me at four thirty this morning and said that he was having a lot of pain and wanted me to come over."

I bumped his bed with considerable vigor. "Damnit, John. I told you to not upset your family. Don't get me wrong, I want you to talk with Mary about your pain, as well as your fears and anxieties, too. But do it when she is here; don't do it over the phone. Put yourself in Mary's position. If she were in the hospital and called you at four in the morning, how would you react? You would be panicky until you could see for yourself that she was okay. By the same token, if Mary calls from home to see how you are, you answer that you are fine. Don't ever upset her on the phone again. Is that clear?"

"I didn't mean to upset her, Tex," John said apologetically.

"I know you didn't mean to, but you did. Patients don't realize how selfish they sometimes are. Don't be so damned self-centered. Be more concerned about your family by being pleasant and cheerful to them. If you're not, I'll stop your pain pills!"

After letting this threat take effect, I said, "I'm only kidding about the pain pills, but I'm not kidding about expecting you to be pleasant to your family. If you're not pleasant, I promise that you will wish you had been. I can be a nice guy, as long as I get my way."

John, obviously embarrassed, did not answer. After I had listened to his lungs and heart and was satisfied with the rest of his examination, I said, "All right, John, let's get going. You have a lot to do. Mary can help you get to the bathroom and shower. I want you to walk in the halls at least six times today, and don't you dare use the urinal again." I was smiling, but my tone was serious. "Now, you both have a good day. We'll see you later this afternoon."

En route to Walter's room, I said to Julie, "It really upsets me to take care of a patient like John. I'm glad we don't have many like him. That kind of patient really drains me."

"We knew he had a poor attitude," Julie said. "It doesn't surprise you that he's acting this way, does it?"

"No, it really doesn't. I'm not worried about his physical recovery. We'll make him get out of bed and walk. I'm much more concerned about his emotional recovery. He's the type of patient who will go home, prop himself up in bed, and demand that his family wait on him hand and foot. He'll want them to bring his meals to him in bed, and he'll have a potty chair in the bedroom so he won't have to get up and walk to the bathroom. He'll do everything in his power to constantly remind his family that he's had open-heart surgery. Don't let me forget to warn Mary this afternoon about not allowing this to happen. If we don't help her prevent it, John will end up being an invalid."

What a different reception we received from Walter. He had showered, shaved, and had already been walking in the halls. "I'm ready to go home!" he announced.

"Let's see," I said, "we did your surgery on Monday, and today is Thursday. That's only three days since your operation. I'm not sure you're quite ready."

Walter quickly challenged me. "How can I be the best patient you've ever had if you won't let me go home? I've done everything you asked me to do, and I've had no complications. I feel great, and I'd do okay at home."

"Walter, you can't go home this soon. Many open-heart patients—in fact almost half of them—develop significant arrhythmias, or irregularities of the heart beat. I want to watch you closely for at least another twenty-four to forty-eight hours to be sure this doesn't happen to you. It can be dangerous if this develops at home. Besides, it would scare the hell out of you and Becky. You both might end up in the Emergency Room. Also, you aren't over the post-op blues yet. Until a patient gets through this phase, I'm usually not willing to send him home."

"You warned me about the blues last night, Tex, and they hit me full force this morning. I woke up really feeling sorry for myself. Becky hadn't called, and you weren't here as early as you were on the other mornings. Then I remembered what you said."

"Walter, let's see how you do today. If you don't have any irregularities of your heart beat, and you feel good this evening, I'll think about letting you go home tomorrow. I wouldn't even consider it if you didn't live in town. Nor would I let you go if I wasn't sure that you'd call me if you had problems. But I think you'll do better at home than here in the hospital. When it gets to the point where all you're doing is sleeping in our bed, taking our pills, and walking in our halls, then it's time to go home. You will be a lot more comfortable in your own bed, won't have to wait for someone to bring your pain pills, and can get outside for some fresh air."

"Tex, tell me what I have to do so I can go home tomorrow, and I'll do it."

"I want you to walk at least eight times in the hall today, more if you're up to it. Begin to walk farther each time, but don't overdo it. I don't want you to get so tired you can't get up the rest of the day. We'll do some blood tests and get another chest X-ray and electrocardiogram. If these look okay, I'll consider sending you home in the next couple of days."

"You're sure you won't let me go this morning? Becky could

be here to pick me up in thirty minutes," Walter persisted. He was still trying to con me. "If I can't go today, can I go tomorrow?"

"We'll discuss it again this evening, but I'm not going to make any promises."

The difference in the progress between Walter and John was striking. John, with his two bypasses, was reluctant to even get up on his own. Walter was ready to go home, although he had undergone a seven-bypass procedure. Their surgeries had been less than twenty-four hours apart. Difference in attitude was responsible, since all other things appeared to be equal, including the fact that Walter and John were about the same age.

While I was finishing the chart work, Julie called to tell me that an emergency had come in and our surgery was going to be delayed about an hour. I went down to the Waiting Room to see Jackie. She was surprised to see me. It was almost 7:40 and she expected me to be in the OR with Dick.

"Jackie, there's going to be a delay. Dick is fine. They had an emergency surgery this morning and are just now finishing. The staff that scrubs on the open-hearts is busy with the emergency. I just wanted to let you know that we're running behind schedule."

"I'm so glad you told me. I don't mind the delay, especially if someone else needs help."

"We probably won't get Dick into the OR until around eight thirty, and it might be later. I'll call you when we do, so don't worry about a thing until you hear from me. The rest of the schedule will be as I told you last night. I'll also call when we have all the lines and tubes in and Dick is asleep. A nurse will make all the other calls."

It was almost 9:30 before we finally got Dick into OR 16. I made the call to Jackie, then started the line in his artery. When he was asleep and all the rest of the lines were in, I called again to let her know that Dick had tolerated the induction of anesthesia well.

We made the leg incision at 10:30. After removing the vein from ankle to groin, we turned to the chest for the tedious portion of Dick's surgery. Fortunately, we were able to get through the sternum without significant complications. With a "virgin" open-heart, it usually takes only a few seconds to cut through the breastbone. In Dick's case, it took almost an hour to open the sternum and dissect the heart away from its sac. The adhesions were dense, but I managed to avoid serious injury to his heart, the complication I feared most at this point in his operation.

During surgery, the promised calls were made to Jackie. It was a little after three when the last dressings were applied and the final phone call was made. Since Dick's was a re-do, it had taken longer than Walter's.

The anesthesiologist on Dick's case was excellent, and I always enjoy working with him. His expertise in administering the anesthetic was evident even before we left OR 16. Dick was already able to open his eyes, nod his head, and move his hands and feet. It was a relief to know so soon that there was no evidence of stroke.

My fear of stroke and the anxiety of waiting to see each patient move all extremities after surgery reminds me of an incident during my second year of residency. I was a junior resident on the open-heart team. One day we had a patient who just wouldn't wake up following surgery. We applied painful stimuli, yelled at him, and did everything we could think of to try to get him to move. We knew the longer he remained unresponsive, the greater the probability he had suffered a stroke.

Finally, totally exasperated, the chief resident walked up to the bedside, and shouted, "Mr. Jones, this is St. Peter! Open your eyes!" Mr. Jones's eyes flew open. Everyone in the room burst out laughing, vastly relieved to know that our patient hadn't suffered the much feared stroke. I'm not sure I would ever resort to such a drastic measure, but I'm not opposed to keeping it in mind. It certainly was effective on that occasion.

16

DICK'S doing fine, Jackie. He's awake and moves everything, so there's no evidence of stroke. He's bleeding minimally and came off the pump easily, which means that he didn't have a significant heart attack during surgery. We may have gotten a late start, but everything went very well once we got through all the scar tissue."

"I know the delay couldn't have been prevented," Jackie said. "It was still a very long day, but the phone calls were a great help."

Before taking Jackie to see Dick, we stopped at the doorway so that I could explain again about the tubes, lines, and equipment. As we approached his bed, I said to Dick, "You smiled when Jackie came in, didn't you?"

The plastic breathing tube prevented him from answering, but he acknowledged Jackie's presence by nodding his head and squeezing her hand. He made a definite effort to smile.

"Dick, are you having much pain?" I asked.

Again he nodded.

"Good! I *want* you to hurt. I want you to hurt so much that you won't ever want another cigarette." He held up his hands as if to surrender. "I may leave that tube down your windpipe for a week as a constant reminder, as well as to prevent you from smoking. Do you promise you'll never smoke again?" I hoped I was getting my point across about the dangers of smoking.

Jackie chimed in. "You won't be the only one kicking his bed. I'll kick it too if I catch him smoking. I don't ever want to go through this again." She looked at Dick, "Next time you can sit out there while I go through surgery." Their children echoed her sentiments.

I told Jackie how pleased I was with Dick's progress. I felt reasonably certain that we would be able to get the tube out of his windpipe and get him up fairly soon.

In my experience, most re-do patients do much better with their second operation. The experience can be compared to a woman having her second baby. It usually is easier because she knows what to expect. The same holds true with open-heart surgery. The operation doesn't hurt any less the second time, but patients just know how to prepare themselves.

On evening rounds we removed the tube from Dick's windpipe and stood him at the bedside. I told him about the importance of coughing. He grabbed a pillow, clutched it to his chest, and demonstrated an excellent cough effort. I had little doubt that he would do well from now on.

When we reached 8-West, Julie and I saw Charles walking with Grace in the hall. A nurse had the chest tubes and the container into which they drained in one hand and was assisting Grace with the other.

Grace greeted us with spirit. "Hi, Tex and Julie. Don't you think I'm doing pretty well for an old lady who is almost sixty-nine?

"You're super. If you were doing any better and we had those tubes out, it would be hard to justify keeping you in the hospital."

"But we'd hate to give you up this soon," Julie said.

The four of us escorted Grace back to her room and to bed.

After listening to her heart and lungs, I checked the amount of drainage from the chest tubes. "Grace, you're still having a little more drainage than I like to see. I think we ought to leave the tubes in until tomorrow morning."

"That's fine, Tex. I'm a little tender where the tubes go through the skin into my stomach, but they're not so bad. Whatever you decide is fine with me."

John was next. His attitude was somewhat better this evening, but still far from ideal. From the very beginning, when he was undergoing evaluation for a possible heart attack in the Coronary Care Unit, he had exhibited "denial of illness." He would not leave his oxygen on, continually got out of bed against orders, and wanted to go to the lounge to smoke. Since surgery, he continued to be uncooperative with the nurses, but in the opposite direction. Now, he almost had to be forced to do anything for himself.

"Hi, Mary. Has John been more pleasant today?"

"He's been better. I think he's beginning to get your message. He got up, took a shower, and shaved this morning."

John had managed a somewhat forced smile when we came through the door. Purposely, I had ignored him. I knew that he was okay from a medical standpoint and I was much more concerned about how he was treating Mary. Finally I spoke directly to him. "How are you feeling, John?"

"I hurt all over!"

"I didn't tell you that you weren't going to hurt. Husky patients seem to have more pain than patients who aren't as muscular, and this goes for both men and women. The more muscular you are, the more your muscles pull on your chest incision when you cough, sit up, or move about. You're probably going to be miserable for the next four to six weeks, so prepare yourself. It will be much worse for you until you begin to accept the fact that you're going to have pain."

Turning to Mary, I said, "Mary, I hate to see you spend your entire day here. John ought to be able to get in and out of bed by himself. The more you do for him, the more inclined he will be to stay in bed and use you. When he goes home, he will do everything he can to perpetuate his 'invalid' status. You probably feel you are showing your love and concern by doing everything for him, but actually you're hurting him in the long run. Remember, his heart is better now than before we operated on him. Those blockages have been there for months and you didn't wait on him hand and foot before surgery, did you? There's no reason to wait on him now. When he goes home, I expect him to dress himself and come to the table for meals. He is to get up every morning, take a shower, comb his hair, and shave. Don't you or the kids make a 'cardiac cripple' out of him."

"Yes, I know what you're saying. Before the surgery I wouldn't have believed you. But this morning, while John was taking his shower, I went to the cafeteria to get a cup of coffee. I met the wife of the man you operated on Monday. When she told me that her husband was doing everything on his own and was ready to go home, I could hardly believe it. When I learned how much faster her husband had progressed than John, I worried that I was partly to blame for not making him do more for himself."

"Mary," Julie said, "that's the same man I took you down to see in the ICU Monday night. John must want to change his attitude before he will do as well as Walter. No one can force him to change."

After examining John and answering other questions, I said, "Tomorrow is your third post-op day. The first three days are the worst; it should get better after that."

"Well, I hope *something* starts getting better. It can't get any worse." We left his room with this sarcastic reply resounding in our ears.

When Walter saw us, he immediately resumed his efforts to secure my permission for an early discharge. "I was afraid you weren't going to come by tonight. I wanted to ask you if I could go down to the cafeteria for supper. I'm getting tired of eating in this room."

"That's a sure sign it's getting close to the time for going home. When patients start complaining about the food, how long it takes to get pain pills, or the noise in the hospital, it's usually time to get them out of here."

Becky said, "If he doesn't need to be here, I'd just as soon have him at home. He's doing better than I am. If you'll let him go, I'm ready to take him."

"Okay," I said. "If he does well tonight, I'll let him go first thing in the morning. Try to be here around eight. Julie and I will talk with you about what he can and can't do when he goes home. I'll check with his referring physician to be sure he thinks it's okay for Walter to be discharged this soon. If it isn't, I'll let Walter know tonight."

"What about these stitches?" Walter asked. "Are you going to take them out before I leave the hospital, or will they come out later? Does it hurt when you take them out?"

"We'll take them out when you come to the office on Tuesday. To answer your second question, no it really doesn't hurt. It may be a little uncomfortable, especially where the stitches are buried in the skin around the knee and groin areas. Otherwise, it's not bad."

Whenever I'm asked if it will hurt to have stitches removed, I am reminded of a young man I operated on during my residency. I had sent him home on the fourth day after minor surgery with instructions to come back three days later for suture removal. He had a short incision, and there were not more than seven or eight stitches. When he came back, he asked if it was going to hurt. I said that it was going to hurt like hell, and if I were he, I would bite a bullet. He turned to his girlfriend and asked for a bullet. She handed him one from a .38 Special. That was the last time I ever advised anyone to bite a bullet. Needless to say, I used extreme care while removing his stitches!

"Becky and I have another question. Exactly what is a heart attack?"

"Heart attacks are caused by blockages in the heart arteries. The more muscle that is supplied by a blocked artery, the more severe the heart attack. In other words, if you block off a small artery that feeds only a small amount of muscle, you have a 'light' heart attack. If you block off a very large vessel, which has many branches, all of the muscle supplied by these branches dies. This results in a massive heart attack."

"What causes the blockages?" Becky asked.

"Blockages, or hardening of the arteries, are something that we all have. This is a normal part of getting older, like gray hair and wrinkles. There are certain things that make a significant difference in the speed at which the blockages develop. Some people—and you're one of them, Walter—inherit the ability to develop blockages. When heredity is a factor, a person is more prone to develop blockages at a younger age than someone who did not inherit this trait. I'm assuming that all other factors are equal. Diabetes and high blood pressure certainly promote the rapidity with which blockages occur. These can and should be controlled by medications. Obesity, lack of exercise, and excessive alcohol intake can increase the formation of blockages. Diet is also important. You should be careful about your intake of foods that are high in cholesterol. This includes the conventional breakfast of bacon and eggs, milk, butter, and cream. That doesn't mean you can't eat these foods at all, it just means that you shouldn't have two eggs every morning for breakfast. If you have two eggs once a week, that's not bad. But eating two or three eggs, several strips of bacon, and all the other things every morning can cause problems with blockages."

I edged forward in my chair for emphasis. "I don't think any of these things are nearly as important as cigarette smoking. Patients with a strong family history can take care of their diabetes, control their high blood pressure and weight, and not drink heavily. But if they smoke, that can be much more damaging than all the other things combined. Smoking is absolutely the worst thing you can do, as I told you before.

"Now, what causes the blockages? As a person grows older, the cholesterol and fats that are in the blood begin to be deposited between the inner wall and outer wall of the arteries. This happens to all of us—it's part of aging. The greater the amount of cholesterol and fats that are deposited in the walls of the blood vessels, the more the channel is narrowed. The narrower the channel, the more the blood flow is restricted. Finally, when the narrowing becomes extreme, blood flow becomes inadequate. If this happens in the heart, it causes a heart attack. If it happens in the brain, it causes a stroke. If it happens in the legs, it can cause gangrene. All of the things I've mentioned play a role in the development of hardening of the arteries, but nothing accelerates it like cigarette smoking."

I left St. John's at about 7:30 P.M. We didn't have a pre-op talk to give, since we had nothing on the surgery schedule in the morning. For the first time this week, when my head hit the pillow, I was able to count sheep instead of reviewing coronary arteriograms. But just as I was drifting off, the chill ring of the phone pierced the silence. As I reached for the receiver, fear gripped me. I don't think I will ever get used to a phone ringing at night. Was Dick hemorrhaging? Or was it a problem with Walter, John, or Grace? It was Grace. She had developed atrial fibrillation, and her heart rate had gone up to one hundred sixty. Her blood pressure had dropped some, but she was stable. After giving several orders for medications and notifying her referring physician, I dressed and returned to the hospital. It was 10:50 P.M.

Even though Grace was in no real danger, I tried to be present if a patient developed problems that could be frightening.

"I was doing so well, and now this had to happen," Grace said. "I'm sorry that you had to come back to the hospital. I was just about to turn out the light when my heart suddenly felt as though it was going to jump out of my chest. It started beating so fast that I was really scared. The nurses said they could see the change in my heart rate on the monitor out at the desk. They told me that you were on your way, and I knew things would be okay when you got here."

"Grace, you're not in any danger. We'll have this under control in a little while. Almost half of our open-heart patients develop this rapid heartbeat. It's called atrial fibrillation, which means that the filling chambers of your heart begin to beat very fast, causing the pumping chambers to beat rapidly as well. If the pumping chambers go into fibrillation, that can kill you; but if the filling chambers go into fibrillation, it's not the same kind of problem. Your heart simply beats very fast and at an irregular rate. This is why we had you on Lanoxin, or digitalis, before surgery. This drug will not prevent atrial fibrillation, but will help control it if it does happen.

"The digitalis is used to slow your heart rate. You will probably go in and out of atrial 'fib' several more times before you leave the hospital, so don't be alarmed if it happens again. The nurse has already given you digitalis through your vein, and she'll give you more during the night until it slows your heart rate. I'll call Charles and let him know that you've had this problem and tell him that you're okay."

In less than an hour, Grace's heart had slowed to one hundred twenty. "I'll see you tomorrow. You're going to be okay. Chances are, by morning you'll be back in your regular rhythm."

Now that Grace was no longer anxious, I kissed her goodnight and left.

Many patients adjust their emotional gears only to getting through the surgery. Once through, they feel they have it made. In reality, most problems and complications arise two to five days after surgery, rather than in the OR. When complications do occur, those patients and families who are best prepared adjust more readily. Of the four open-hearts that we had done this week, Grace was the best prepared to handle a complication. Fortunately, her case was one of the least dangerous.

17

WALTER, dressed in slacks and a sports coat, was at the nurses' station. He was already asking when Julie and I would arrive to dismiss him.

We walked him back to his room where Becky was packing his things. She had already gotten one of the discharge carts and had it half filled with flowers and other mementos of his hospital stay.

"Hi, Becky," I said. "Looks like this is the big day! Are you ready to take this guy home?"

"I certainly am!" she replied enthusiastically. "We've got two little girls who can hardly wait to see their Daddy. You would have thought last night was Christmas Eve. They came running in every hour, asking if it was time to go get Daddy."

"Well, let's see if we can't get their Christmas present to them a couple of months early."

I sat down with Becky and Walter in preparation for routine "going home" instructions, but first asked, "Walter, do you have any questions?"

"Yeah. What's causing the popping sensation in my chest, and what about the swelling of my right leg?"

"Your breastbone is held together with heavy, stainless-steel wires. They are in there permanently, and will never need to be removed. The popping feeling is caused by the edges of the breastbone rubbing together. The sternum is made up of a central, soft portion that is called bone marrow, and the outer layers are made up of hard bone. The popping occurs when these outer edges of hard bone shift against each other. You will have this sensation for about eight to ten weeks. Only when your sternum has completely healed will the popping sensation stop.

"Your question about swelling is a good one. It is not because the vein was removed. You have lots of veins left that will drain the blood from your leg, so the removal of one does not cause significant problems. This vein is the same one that doctors strip out for varicose veins.

"You have swelling because the long incision from your goin to your ankle has cut across lymph channels. When a woman has her breast removed, the lymph glands under her arm are removed. This usually causes massive swelling of the arm after surgery. Because of the long incision, you have the same problem in your leg. The divided lymph channels do not allow for lymph drainage from your leg. When new drainage routes are re-established, the problems with swelling will disappear. You will notice that the swelling is worse at the end of the day after you've been on your feet or sitting for long periods of time. This is because of gravity. You will also notice that the swelling is almost completely gone each morning. When you are lying down, the effect of gravity is lessened. The support hose you have been wearing will help cut down on the swelling, and I recommend that you get some men's support hose and wear two stockings on the right leg and one on the left. This double thickness of support will help keep the swelling down. If the swelling increases so that you have problems getting your shoes on, we can give you water pills to get rid of some of the fluid.

"Now about going home. Your regular doctor will tell you about your diet and the medications he wants you to take, and give you instructions about the things you can and can't do. From my standpoint as your surgeon, I have very few restrictions. I do not want you to do stupid things, like climbing up on the roof to clean the leaves out of the gutters, or up in a tree to get the cat down. Don't get up on cabinets or ladders to change a light bulb. In other words, don't get up in high places where you could fall. It's okay to go up and down stairs, because if you stumble, each step breaks your fall as you bump to the bottom. Falling from six feet up off a ladder is different; there is nothing to break your fall. It will take about ten weeks for your breastbone to heal solidly; after that, you can do anything you want.

"Many people ask when they can drive. I don't want you to drive until, in all good conscience, you are able to react quickly if a child runs out in front of you. This means you have to be able to slam on the breaks and swerve. If you have to put the brakes on carefully and slowly, because of tenderness in your leg incision, that's not good enough. Before you can drive, you have to be able to slam on the brakes with your right foot without wincing from pain. You are guarding against pain in the upper part of your chest incision, and will tend to hold your neck rigid and turn your body, rather than just turning your head, to look to either side. When you can turn your head from side to side without guarding against the pain in your neck, you can drive. Finally, you must be able to swerve the steering wheel with both arms. You shouldn't drive as long as you have to hold your hands in your lap and turn the wheel from that position because it is painful to raise your arms. Becky can take you to an empty parking lot or to some lonely road to give you your driving test. When you are safe, to her satisfaction, then you can drive.

"Another rule: you should never take pain pills in anticipation of pain. In other words, if you go out and work in the yard and you begin having incisional pain, don't take a pain pill to relieve the discomfort, and then continue working. Take the pain pill and quit. Pain is your warning signal to stop doing something that might be harmful to you. Don't mask that signal with narcotics. Athletes do more harm to themselves when they are injured in a game, go over to the sidelines for an injection of a deadening medication into a knee joint or ankle, and then return to the game. Pain meds remove your body's own natural protective mechanisms. Like the athlete, you can harm yourself when you do anything physically strenuous under the cover of pain medications.

"I expect you to be walking approximately one mile at a time within four to six weeks, but work up to this gradually. Walk a quarter of a mile three or four times a day to build up your stamina. Don't go out and walk a mile tomorrow, then be so tired that you end up spending the rest of the day in bed. I don't want you to ever exhaust yourself. This might be a problem at first because you don't yet know your limitations. The best guideline is to push yourself to the point of being a little tired, but not to the point of exhaustion.

"I don't want you sitting for longer than thirty minutes at any one time for the next four to six weeks. If you're watching TV, get up and walk around during every other commercial break. If you're on a plane, go to the lavatory several times during the flight. The other passengers might think you have a bladder problem, but at least you won't be developing clots in your legs. It's okay to take trips in the car, but every fifty miles or so, you should stop, get out, and take a brisk walk.

"Otherwise, Walter, you can do anything you feel like doing. The edges of your breastbone rubbing together will cause enough discomfort to discourage you from doing anything you shouldn't be doing. I don't want you moving refrigerators or heavy furniture. But if you don't have pain, you aren't going to tear up anything that I've done, as long as you haven't been taking pain pills to mask the pain.

"You can have intercourse. Obviously you're going to have to find a position that is comfortable for you, but I'm sure you will. Another warning, don't take pain pills before intercourse because you expect discomfort in your chest or leg incisions. The pills may greatly affect your sexual performance by dulling normal sensations. Therefore, you may not have a satisfactory sex life as long as you're on pain pills.

"Becoming discouraged about your general progress is probably the biggest problem you will have to face. This is a normal reaction to the seemingly inordinate length of time it will take you to regain your strength. You'll feel that you should be regaining strength much faster. Let me tell you a story that will help you understand why it takes so long. There was a study done a couple of years ago at a medical center in which first-year medical students were put on a treadmill. These young men went almost twenty minutes at full speed and with maximum elevation of the treadmill. They were then put to bed. Meals, bed pan, and anything else they needed were brought to them. They were kept flat in bed for three days, then they were gotten up, exercised on a treadmill, and sent back to their classes. In the evenings these students jogged, played football, or engaged in whatever form of exercise they usually did. Every couple of days they would be retested on the treadmill. The amazing finding of this study was that it took them three weeks to achieve the same level of performance on the treadmill that they had before they were put to bed. That's seven days of recuperation for every one day they were in bed. Those students were not thirty-nine years old, had not undergone open-heart surgery, had not been under an anesthetic, or been in pain; they were healthy young men. Because of your age, the fact that you underwent surgery, and you didn't get adequate rest as a result of post-op discomfort, it will take you ten days for every one day that you were in bed to regain your strength. This includes the days you were in the hospital last week for your heart cath.

"Now you can understand why I got you up so soon after surgery; I didn't want you to lose your strength by lying in bed. The longer you're in bed, the longer you will have to pay the price. Since you were in the hospital three days last week for your cath and five days this week, it will take you approximately eighty days to regain your strength. That's almost three months, so don't get discouraged. It will come back by exercising, not by lying around or eating."

"I'm really glad you explained all this. I feel fine now, but I know I'd get discouraged if I pooped out trying to do the things I did a month ago."

"Walter, I haven't ever discharged an open-heart patient this soon after surgery. I usually keep them for seven to ten days, and sometimes longer, especially if they live out of town. I'm letting you go only because you've done so well and it's to your advantage to go home. You and Becky can call me anytime if you have problems or questions. You have my card, and my home phone number is on it. Don't hesitate to use it. Julie or I will probably call in the next couple of days to see how you're doing, otherwise we will see you in the office on Tuesday to remove your stitches."

As Becky stood up, I put my arms around her. "Thanks for being so understanding of Julie and me. I know there were times you probably wished we had been here to answer questions, but you always waited patiently until we made rounds. We appreciate your thoughtfulness."

Then Julie hugged Walter. "We couldn't have asked for a better patient," she said.

"I've got something to say," Walter announced. "I probably dreaded coming into the hospital and having surgery more than any patient you have ever taken care of. But I've got to admit that it has truly been an enjoyable experience. I've learned a lot about myself and about consideration for others. I would never have believed that anyone could say that they enjoyed going through surgery, but I honestly can."

"Walter, you've been a superb patient," I said. "Initially, I was a little worried about your attitude on Sunday night, but once we finished the pre-op talk, I was sure that you would do well. You did everything I asked you to do, and more. You've been a real pleasure to take care of, and I wish you the very best of luck."

"Thanks, Tex. That means a lot coming from you." Nervously he ran a hand through his hair. "I'm not sure how to say this, because I don't know how I'm supposed to thank the man who saved my life." His voice cracked with emotion. Tears filled his eyes.

I knew what Walter was trying to say, and I felt uncomfortable and embarrassed.

Walter extended his right hand, and as our hands gripped, he put his arm around my neck for a moment. "I guess this is the only way I know how, Tex. Thanks!"

"I know what you're trying to say, but you don't need to thank me. Thank Him," I said, pointing upward. "He's the one who brought you through this. Maybe Julie and I can take some credit for helping you develop the proper attitude, but as far as I'm concerned, getting well was ninety percent up to you. You did a beautiful job, and you don't need to thank us. You did the hard part. Julie and I just had it rough Monday morning."

Walter wiped his eyes. "I feel stupid crying like this."

"You're likely to cry fairly easily for some time after surgery. Less than four days ago, I stopped your heart for ninety-one minutes; you can't forget how close you were to death. A lot of things in your life will take on a different meaning now. You'll appreciate Becky and your kids more than you ever have. Your priorities will change drastically; things that used to mean a great deal to you may no longer seem important. When you get home, I want you to treat Becky and the kids with just as much consideration as you did while you were here in the hospital."

To Becky, I said lightheartedly, "If he isn't nice to you and the kids, kick his bed. If that doesn't work, hide his pain pills and don't give them to him until he starts being pleasant again. Best of luck to both of you. Don't hesitate to call if you need me. Thanks again, Walter, for being such a great patient. Start thinking about going back to work. It's important that patients set goals for their recovery. We'll talk about this when you come to the office on Tuesday."

As Julie and I walked down the hall, we could not help feeling a sense of loss. We would miss Walter. He was a patient who had become a friend.

18

I HAD SPENT more time with John than with any other patient this week, yet he had failed to respond. At this stage in his recovery he was not motivated to do well and was still selfishly focusing on his own needs, not concerned with how this was affecting his family. But I would keep working with John. Somehow, I would find a way to convince him that his illness was just as painful to Mary and the children as it was to him. His slow rate of recovery would give me ample opportunity to discover a solution.

Earlier this morning, just before our visit, Grace had converted back into a regular rhythm. In all probability she would go in and out of atrial fibrillation several more times before stabilizing into her normal rhythm.

After completing rounds, we arrived in the office a little before eleven. Sylvia asked about Grace, and was surprised to learn that Walter had gone home. She was pleased to hear that Dick was doing well enough to be transferred to 8-West.

With two new consultations to see, Julie and I returned to St. John's, hoping to finish rounds early enough so that I could attend Monte's football scrimmage. Both of the consults were on possible candidates for bypass surgery. After reviewing their films several times, we saw Carl first. He was a sixty-two-year-old man who had suffered a heart attack two years earlier and had had no problems until about a month ago. He had then developed angina with strenuous activity and, during the past six days, with even moderate exertion. His coronary arteriograms revealed significant blockages in five of the major branches of his coronary arteries. We discussed the cath findings with him, along with the alternatives of continued medical management or surgical intervention, and described the risks of each. He chose surgery and was scheduled for Monday morning. We arranged to meet with his wife and children for the pre-op talk Sunday evening at eight.

Bill, the other consultation, was a forty-six-year-old man who had suffered four previous heart attacks, two of them within the last three months. Since his last attack, he had noted increasing shortness of breath with the least amount of physical activity. It was necessary for him to use two pillows at night in order to keep from being awakened by shortness of breath. Angina attacks were occurring frequently, sometimes arousing him from sleep. He could obtain relief only if he placed one or two nitroglycerine tablets under his tongue. Because he had been in the hospital so many days during the past three months and because he was afraid of being hospitalized again, he had put off calling his physician. Then one night, the pain had become so intense that he couldn't sleep. When he did notify his doctor, he was immediately hospitalized and the subsequent arteriograms were performed.

"Bill," I said, "I'm Tex and this is my nurse, Julie. I'm the heart surgeon that your doctor asked to come by and see you."

Bill put out his cigarette, sat up on the side of the bed, and shook my hand. "Hi, Doc. This is my wife, Deedie." We got the "Doc" thing straightened out, and I pulled out my prescription pad and drew a picture of Bill's heart and its arteries. "This is what your heart and its blood vessels looked like many years ago."

Then I drew in the numerous changes that had taken place in Bill's once healthy heart. "This is what your heart looks like now. As you can see, two of your major heart arteries are completely occluded, and the third is ninety percent blocked. You've developed tiny detour vessels around these obstructions, and these supply all of the blood that your heart gets. The blockages are a big enough problem, but your real problem is the fact that your heart is now dilated much beyond its normal size.

"Your heart, instead of beating normally like this"—I interlocked my fingers and squeezed the palms together repeatedly to demonstrate the normal pumping mechanism of a heart—"now beats like this." I put both hands up as if I were holding a large cantaloupe and gently flexed my fingers, not moving any one finger more than a half inch. "Your heart beats like a bowl of Jell-o; it just sits there, barely moving.

"Your heart has been so badly damaged from your previous heart attacks that even if we bypassed your blocked arteries, the small amount of normal heart muscle that you have left would not be able to squeeze any better than it does now. A heart attack results in the death of heart muscle, which then becomes scar tissue. This scar tissue can never regenerate into what it once was. You have so little reserve muscle left that I don't believe I can get you through surgery. I have to feel that I can get someone through surgery before I will operate on him or her."

"What you're trying to tell me," Bill said, "is that my heart is so bad you can't operate on it." He reached for a Kleenex and blotted his eyes. Deedie began to cry; Julie knelt beside her.

"Bill can't go on this way," Deedie sobbed. "We knew his heart was bad, but we hoped it wasn't this bad."

"Doc, what——" Bill started to say.

"Don't call me that, Bill. I told you earlier to call me Tex. Whether I operate on you or not, I want you to leave this hospital as a friend of mine."

"I'm just going to have to learn to live like this, right, Tex?"

"Yes, Bill. In essence that's what I'm saying. Quite a few things can be done. We have given you medications to make your heart muscle contract better. The water pills will help get rid of the excess fluid that's causing your symptoms of heart failure. But in my opinion, you are simply not a candidate for coronary artery bypass surgery."

They were silent for a few moments. Then Deedie said, "Do you know what a tremendous blow this is to Bill? Some of his friends have had the bypass surgery. This is what finally convinced him to have the heart catheterization. His doctor and I have tried to get him to come in for a heart cath ever since his second heart attack, but he never would. If he had come in then, would he have been a candidate for the operation?"

"Anything that I say would be speculation. It's easy to be a 'Monday morning quarterback' and say what *should* have been done. I'm not going to criticize Bill for what he did or didn't do, or what he should or shouldn't have done. I'm sure he realizes now that it would have been best if he had come in after his second heart attack. But suppose he had undergone the cath, had the surgery, and then died on the table. If this had happened, your feelings would be completely different from what they are today. He's had seven or eight good years since his second heart attack and only recently began to get into trouble."

"I still can't help feeling that if he had come through the surgery seven or eight years ago, we wouldn't be where we are today," Deedie argued. "At least with surgery, we would know we had tried."

"You may be right, Deedie," I conceded. In order to avoid further discussion about what might have been, I asked if there were any other questions.

"Why do I wake up at night short of breath?" Bill asked.

"This happens because your heart has been injured so badly

that it is no longer pumping as well as it should and has become enlarged. Since your heart is no longer able to function properly, blood backs up into your lungs and feet. When you lie down at night, fluid that has accumulated in your ankles during the day shifts to your lungs. You wake up because of the sensation of drowning caused by this accumulation of fluid in your lungs. This is called congestive heart failure. You get relief by sitting up so that gravity can help pull this fluid out of your lungs back into your feet."

I concluded by saying, "I know what you've heard this afternoon has been very disheartening. After you've had a chance to talk together, you may have some other questions. Julie and I will come by tomorrow morning.

"Bill, you've been doing pretty well until recently. I feel sure your doctor can relieve some of your angina and make you more comfortable with medications." I respected him for his courageous reaction to my devastating news.

"Yes," he said in a resigned tone. "But I was so hopeful that you would be able to operate. In the last three weeks, I haven't been able to do anything without running out of breath or developing chest pain. I don't think I could work now, but I've *got* to work. I have a family to support and four kids to raise."

I was too upset to speak for several seconds. Finally, I was able to say, "Keep fighting, Bill, and don't give up. We'll see you in the morning."

Deedie was sniffling, and Julie was trying to comfort her. Kneeling down, I took Deedie's hands. "Deedie, it's going to be okay. They will get Bill on the proper medications, and that will help him a great deal."

"Tex, I know that there are two types of patients who are turned down for heart surgery. One is the patient who does not need it, and the other is too big a risk. I had a feeling yesterday that Bill might fall in the second category. You've just confirmed my fear."

"If I felt there was any chance that I could get Bill through the surgery and help him, I would operate on him. But I don't feel I can. If it would ease your mind, another heart surgeon could look at Bill's cath films."

"That won't be necessary," Deedie said. "When the doctor talked to me after Bill's cath, he doubted that surgery would be possible. But he wanted to leave the final decision up to you."

As Julie and I walked slowly down the hall, we passed John's room. We were both depressed about Bill, who was now a true "cardiac cripple." His prognosis was dismal; if he lived a year, he would never be able to do more than simple chores around his farm. I was in no mood to face John, that is until I overheard a nurse saying, "You have to get up and walk because that's what Tex ordered."

John's reply got my attention. "I've already been up two or three times today. I don't give a damn what Tex says. If I don't feel like getting up, I'm not going to."

I burst into John's room with fire in my eyes.

"What's this crap about not walking? If I give orders that you are to get up and walk, you ask the nurse how often, when, and how far. I just finished telling a patient that he was not a candidate for surgery. In all probability he has nothing to look forward to but a slow, progressive, downhill course until he dies. This man would give anything to go through the pain that you're complaining about. He almost begged me to operate. But I had to say no because I did not feel I could get him through it. His heart is just too bad. He has suffered multiple heart attacks, and there's too much scar tissue. You have an excellent heart. You've come through surgery, you're doing fine, but you don't appreciate it!"

I bumped John's bed. "You get up out of that damn bed and walk. You walk every time anyone asks you to. If I have to come down here and walk you myself, I will. You may not know it, but half the people die with their first heart attack. There were no warnings for them, like you had. They didn't get a chance to go through surgery and have their blocked arteries bypassed; they just died. Another group of patients have multiple heart attacks and end up with so much scar tissue that they don't have a heart that can function adequately as a pump. These people die slowly of heart failure. You had some warning, and we were able to bypass your blocked vessels. You ought to be damn grateful.

"Your selfishness and self-centered attitude make me sick. It's time you started thinking about somebody other than yourself. As long as you're a patient of mine, you'll not act like this again. You'll do exactly as the nurses ask, and you will not say one word to Mary, the nurses, or Julie and me about how much pain and discomfort you're having, without a smile. I'm almost tempted to take you in to meet the man I just spoke to, and let you moan and groan to him about your pain and discomfort. If you realized what he's got to look forward to, I'll bet your attitude would change!"

I turned my back on John and walked to the window. It took some time for me to cool off. Finally, I was able to face him. "When I was a junior in high school, the first-string quarterback got hurt, and I took over his position. The coaches were on my back every time I made an error. They rode me for days. Finally it got to the point that I wasn't sure that I could take it any more, and I told them so. The head coach told me something I'll always remember: 'As long as I'm on your tail, you don't have to worry. You need to worry when I'm not on your tail, because then I've given up on you.' John, the same applies to you. I'm tempted to tell the nurses, Mary, and the rest of the people involved with your case to get the hell out of your room and let you be. If you want to get up and do the things that will help you get well, you will. You'd be on your own. But I'm not going to do that because we all care about you. We all want you to get well, but you're not going to upset the nurses, and you're damn sure not going to destroy your family. Is that clear?"

"Hey, Tex, I didn't mean to upset the nurses or Mary. I've been up several times today, and I didn't feel like getting up again right now. I was going to walk later."

"Well, maybe you were, and maybe you weren't. It just infuriates me to see someone who isn't any more appreciative of making it through surgery than you are. Mary, I think John needs some time alone. Why don't you leave and come back in the morning? John can think about what's happened this afternoon."

Later I said to Julie, "You probably feel I was too harsh with John."

"No, Tex," Julie answered. "I might have handled him differently, but I know what you were trying to do, and I agree."

"Whenever I'm faced with a problem patient like John, I remember the advice Ann Landers once gave to parents: 'Without discipline there can be no respect; without respect there can be no love.' A similar situation has to exist between me and my patients. I know I set high expectations for each patient. If they want me as their physician, then they must have the self-discipline to attain these goals. When this is present, there will be mutual respect and the rest will fall into place."

After dictating the consult on Bill, and writing a note in his chart, we went to see Grace. Charles met us at the door and told us that Grace was somewhat confused. I explained to him that this phenomenon is common, especially in patients who are deprived of sleep for several consecutive days. I reminded Charles that Grace had not slept the night of surgery, because of the frequency with which she was checked during the night. Nor had she slept last night because the nurses were in and out after she developed atrial fibrillation. Anyone will become confused if deprived of sleep long enough, but the confusion is temporary. The only treatment for it is adequate sleep. One of the reasons I get my patients out of the ICU so soon is to establish them in a quiet room where sleep is less interrupted. We would have been okay with Grace had she not developed problems last night. I suggested to Charles that he help Grace walk at least twice more this evening. I hoped that the walks would tire her, helping her to sleep better.

Our next stop was Dick's room. When we walked in, Dick and Jackie told us they had a surprise. Neither Julie nor I were in the mood for pranks, but we went along with their request to close our eyes and hold out our hands. When we opened our eyes, each of us was holding a brown paper sack. Inside each sack was a T-shirt. The front of mine was adorned with a smile bedecked with a mustache. Below this were the words "Smile—or I'll Kick Your Bed." Julie's "smile" was identical to mine but without the mustache. Below her smile were the words "Smile— or He'll Kick Your Bed." We both laughed so hard that our sides hurt.

Monte had invited Julie to his scrimmage, so she met us at our home. Dressed in Levis, Sylvia, Gary, Julie, and I got ready to leave for the game. Before doing so, I placed a call to Walter to see how his first afternoon home had gone. He was elated with his continued progress and happy to be home with his family.

We arrived at the football field just before the scrimmage began. The opposing team got the ball first, and Monte made the tackle on the second play. In my excitement, I almost missed the message over my beeper to call St. John's Emergency Room, immediately.

Monte's scrimmage ended for us after only two plays.

19

THE Emergency Room call concerned a seventy-two-year-old man who had arrived at the ER in shock. He had the signs and symptoms of a ruptured abdominal aortic aneurysm. Over the phone I had given numerous orders to the nurses, including an order to type and cross-match for transfusions. The OR had been notified, and Helen and Laura were called in for the surgery.

Twelve minutes after leaving Monte's scrimmage, we entered the Emergency Room. I was still dressed in Levis, and hoped the family would understand our casual attire. In the Treatment Room, James was conscious and surprisingly alert. He had no obtainable blood pressure, nor could I feel any pulses. This freakish finding of mental alertness in the absence of audible blood pressure or palpable pulses occurs occasionally when a patient is in profound shock, usually from massive blood loss. The heart monitor showed a rapid pattern. The fact that this man was alert meant that enough blood was getting to his brain, but the absence of urine output indicated that his kidneys were not receiving an adequate blood supply. This was an ominous sign. I examined his abdomen, and agreed with the diagnosis of a ruptured aneurysm of the abdominal aorta.

"James, we think that the severe pain in your back is caused by the rupture of the large artery in your belly. That's why you're so distended. If you're agreeable, we're going to take you to surgery immediately."

"Do whatever you have to do, but please do something soon. My back is killing me. It feels as though someone has run a sword through me."

"We'll do what we can. Is your family here with you?"

"Yes, my wife and daughter followed the ambulance. They should be outside somewhere."

"You'll be moved up to surgery in a few minutes, but we'll let you see your family first."

I dreaded having to talk to families under these circumstances. There simply wasn't time to help them deal with the cold facts of what I needed to tell them—no time for a scheduled pre-op talk when Julie and I could take them along at their own pace. We found James's wife Elaine and their daughter Phyllis in the ER Waiting Room and sat down to prepare them as best we could. The two women were almost in a state of shock themselves.

"Elaine," I said, "we've got big problems. I think James has blown a hole in the large artery in his belly. This artery is called the abdominal aorta. Two things can happen to blood vessels as a person gets older. Usually, they develop blockages that cause the arteries to become narrowed. But sometimes, as the wall of the blood vessel becomes diseased, instead of narrowing, it weakens and the artery enlarges. When this occurs, it's called an aneurysm. When you develop an aneurysm of the abdominal aorta, there is a high risk that the artery will rupture. I think this is what has happened to James."

I picked up a Kleenex box, turned it over, and made a drawing of what I was trying to explain (see Figure 7). "We need to remove the part of the artery that has ruptured, the aneurysm, and replace it with a plastic artery."

Figure 7 · Jᴀᴍᴇs's Aɴᴇᴜʀʏsᴍ

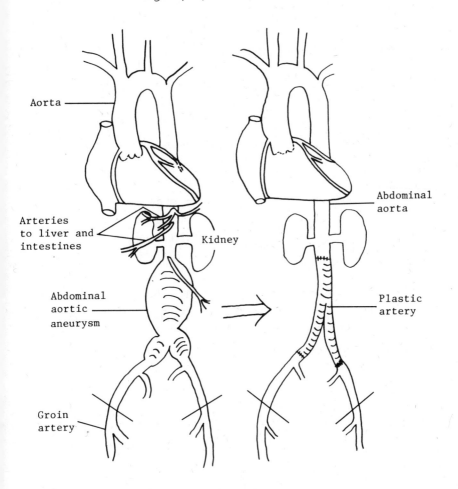

Aorta

Abdominal
aorta

Arteries
to liver and
intestines

Kidney

Abdominal
aortic
aneurysm

Plastic
artery

Groin
artery

"How long do you think Daddy has had this?" Phyllis asked.

"I don't know for sure, but I would guess for a couple of years."

Elaine told me that James had been complaining about his back for the last ten days to two weeks. "Do you suppose this artery was causing that problem?"

"There is a real possibility that it was. The artery was probably starting to expand or leak at that time. It would have been much better if we could have operated on him earlier. I feel that anyone who has an abdominal aortic aneurysm that is over two and a half to three inches in diameter should have it removed and replaced with a plastic artery as an elective procedure as soon as the aneurysm is discovered. The risk of this surgery, on an elective basis, is probably in the range of five to eight percent, compared to the ninety-percent risk of operating on someone who had already ruptured this artery. That's what I must talk to you about.

"We need to take him to surgery right now or he's going to bleed to death. There's one problem; he's a seventy-two-year-old man. His chances of getting through surgery are very slim. I hate to put him through the pain of surgery when his chances of ever leaving the hospital are almost zero, unless you are absolutely sure that this is what you want done. The alternative is to keep him comfortable with sedation and let nature take its course."

Without hesitation, Elaine said, "No, we want you to do everything you possibly can to save him. I just wish we had known what was causing the pain ten days ago and had brought him to the hospital, but he wouldn't come."

"Don't look back at what could have been done. Few people realize that this type of back pain is so life-threatening."

I felt an urgency to move ahead. "If you consent to the surgery, then I need to tell you what we're up against. James's blood pressure is so low that we can't even hear it. We're pumping blood and fluids into him as fast as we can, but we still haven't been able to generate enough pressure to feel any pulses. Because of his low blood pressure, he can have a stroke or heart attack at any moment. Even if we get him through the surgery, his blood pressure has been low for so long that he's likely to have permanent kidney failure. Our biggest concern right now is that we'll take him to surgery, open his abdomen, and then not be able to control the bleeding. If this happens, he'll hemorrhage to death in the Operating Room.

"Julie and I want you to know that we're going to do our very best to save him, but we're fighting against terrible odds. As I said earlier, our chances of getting James through the surgery are less than one out of ten. Even if he does survive the surgery, there is a long and difficult recovery period ahead. Getting him through the operation is only the beginning. It's important that you are aware of this."

Elaine and Phyllis nodded their heads in resigned acceptance.

"We'll take you in to see James now. After you've seen him, I suggest that you go to the Surgical Waiting Room on the third floor. Stay there while we're in surgery. I'll have one of the nurses from the OR call you several times during the operation to let you know how we're doing. Good or bad, I'll keep you informed. I have no idea how long the surgery will take. It may be over very quickly if his artery blows out completely and he dies before we can get into his abdomen. Otherwise, it probably will take four to five hours."

With our arms around them, Julie and I took the two women to see James, knowing that it might be the last time they would see him alive. Then we went with James to surgery, changed into scrub clothes, and entered OR 9. In less than five minutes, Helen had efficiently set up the instruments for surgery. Her presence was comforting; no matter what trouble I might find myself in, she could be counted on to hand me the correct instruments. Laura would handle the calls to the family with compassion as well as handle her role of circulating nurse. I felt good about the team that would be giving James his best chance for survival.

James was still alert. Julie held his hand and offered words of encouragement while I left the room to begin my scrub. Laura waited until James was asleep, then applied the antiseptic solution from his upper chest to his knees.

The anesthesiologist had obtained a blood pressure of fifty when James first arrived in the OR, but just after induction of anesthesia his pressure dropped to zero. I knew we were headed for big trouble. I gowned and gloved rapidly and with Helen's help applied the sterile drapes, and picked up a scalpel. By this time Julie had completed her scrub and stood opposite me at James's left side.

Quickly, I made a midline stomach incision from the edge of James's rib cage to his pubic bone. Entering the abdominal cavity, I found a large clot, the size of a football, surrounding the abdominal aorta. A second area of clot, even larger than this, was found behind the left side of the large intestine. Minutes after making the skin incision, I applied a clamp to the abdominal aorta where it enters into the abdomen from the chest. Almost immediately, the anesthesiologist remarked that he could hear a blood pressure of sixty, and was soon able to confirm this by the arterial line he placed in James's wrist artery. In placing the clamp on the aorta so close to the chest we had shut off all blood supply to James's liver, intestines, and, more important, kidneys. But I knew that this was the only way that I could quickly gain control of his bleeding aneurysm.

With the aorta clamped, I moved the intestines out of the way, and entered the area of the aneurysm. The more clot material I removed, the more profuse the bleeding became, despite the clamp that was still in place on the aorta above. The bleeding was coming from the ruptured aneurysm through vessels that detoured around the clamp. This is called back-bleeding or collateral flow.

Then began the real struggle. Solely by feel, I would have to place clamps across the aorta just above and below the ruptured aneurysm. The profuse hemorrhage prevented me from visualizing the aorta. At times the bleeding was so severe that blood ran over the sides of the incision onto our shoes. For several moments I doubted that I would be able to control the hemorrhage.

As the tension mounted, perspiration soaked the front of my cap. Laura frequently mopped my brow to keep perspiration from running down my face into the operating field. Finally, the bleeding ceased with the placement of two clamps above and below the aneurysm. I was able to remove the clamp that had been placed near the chest, re-establishing blood flow to James's liver and kidneys.

"Laura, please call the family," I said, "and let them know that we encountered a great deal of bleeding. Tell them that for a while things looked pretty grim, but right now we have the hemorrhage under control."

During the next fifty minutes we removed the ruptured aneurysm and sewed in a new "plastic artery." It was in the shape of an inverted Y, with the two limbs going to each of the leg arteries. With a clamp still on the aorta just below the kidneys, we had been able to produce a blood pressure of approximately one hundred. This was obtained with massive amounts of transfusions, i.v. fluids, and drugs to stimulate James's heart. Upon removal of the clamps and re-establishment of blood flow to the legs, his blood pressure dropped precipitously. This occurred because the volume of blood required to supply James's whole body, including his pelvic area and legs, was much greater than what was needed to supply his body above the kidneys when the clamp was across the aorta.

We soon had a new problem. There was oozing from the entire plastic artery, all suture lines, and any other tissues that we had cut through while entering the abdomen. Because James had used up most of his clotting factors, including his platelets, trying to form a clot to seal off his ruptured aneurysm, new clot formation was impaired. Two hours later, after replacing the clotting factors as best we could, we finally had some control over the bleeding.

We had made multiple calls to Elaine and Phyllis during the operation, none of which was optimistic. I now asked Laura, "Would you please call the family again, and let them know that James's condition is fair? We're beginning to close the abdomen, but we'll be in surgery at least another hour. Tell them to stay in the Waiting Room. We'll come for them when James is settled in the ICU."

As we started to close the abdomen, I began to think ahead. The real challenge was no longer in the OR, but in getting James through the difficult post-op problems that usually develop in cases like these. Since arriving in the Emergency Room, James had had no urine output. Unless his oozing slowed and his kidneys began to function, I knew that he wouldn't survive another twelve hours.

It was almost one in the morning before we got James to the ICU and felt that he was stable enough so that his family could see him. Entering the Waiting Room, I walked over to Elaine and sat down. Julie sat beside Phyllis.

"James is in the ICU. He's alive. He made it through the surgery, but this doesn't necessarily mean that he's going to be okay. There are several things I need to discuss with you now that we have more time.

"First, James's blood pressure is presently in the range of ninety to one hundred; but this pressure is a result of drugs stimulating his heart. We hope to get him off these drugs during the night.

"My second concern is that he's oozing from everywhere. He's oozing from needle puncture sites, from his abdominal incision, and from his nose and mouth. He's bleeding like this because he's used up all the clotting factors in his blood, trying to seal off the hole in his ruptured artery. We're replacing these clotting factors, but unless he stops oozing, he will continue to use them up as fast as we can give them to him.

"In addition, he has not put out any urine since he was admitted to the hospital. Because his blood pressure was so low, we had to give him massive amounts of transfusions and i.v. fluids. We did this to try to bring his blood pressure back up. All these fluids are now in his body, and if his kidneys don't start working, his system will be overloaded and he will go into heart failure.

"We also have the risk of infection. Whenever a plastic artery is placed in the body, there is the danger of infection. This is especially true when it is placed in an area where there has been a great deal of hemorrhage because blood is an excellent medium for growing bacteria. We have given James antibiotics in an effort to prevent this problem.

"I don't want to paint a bleak picture, but I think it's only fair to tell you that our odds of getting him through this are still in the range of less than one out of ten."

Phyllis nodded, signifying that she was aware of the gravity of my words. "When can we see Daddy?" she asked.

"We'll take you in now, but first let me describe what you will see." I told them about the tube in his windpipe connected to the breathing machine, the i.v. in his neck, the multiple i.v. lines in his arms, and the line in his wrist artery. I also told them that he would look pale and very swollen.

As we approached James's bed, I warned Elaine and Phyllis that he would not know they were there. He was still under the anesthetic. I walked with Elaine to his bedside, and placed his cool, puffy hand in hers. Julie took Phyllis to the opposite side of the bed.

Elaine squeezed her husband's hand. With tear-filled eyes she gazed at the deathly pallor of his face. Only the rhythmic signal from the heart monitor and our reassurances helped her realize that James was indeed still alive.

Elaine turned to leave; she had had enough. Phyllis, with tears running down her cheeks, leaned over and said, "Daddy, it's Mama and me. You're going to be okay. We're praying for you."

When we were seated again in the deserted Waiting Room, I told them what to expect in the hours ahead. "The next eight to twelve hours will be the most critical. Julie and I will be checking with you every hour or so to let you know how things are going. If you want to lie down on the couches, you can. We'll let you know if there are any significant changes."

"If I had gone in there, not knowing what to expect, I would have been very upset," Elaine said. "It's amazing how different someone can look after going through surgery. He doesn't even look like the same person we saw five or six hours ago."

"You know things look pretty bleak, don't you, Elaine?"

Julie and I changed places so that I could talk with Phyllis. "I know that your Mom appreciates you being here. We're going to do everything we can, but I think our chances of getting your Dad through this are almost negligible."

When Julie and I returned to the ICU, James's blood pressure was in the range of one hundred twenty, and he was being weaned off the drugs to stimulate his heart. This was the only good sign. He was continuing to ooze from everywhere; he had put out no urine; the line in his neck, measuring the filling pressure of his right atrium, showed signs of heart failure. In an effort to monitor the pumping ability of his heart more closely, we used a cutdown to place a catheter into the lung artery to directly measure the filling pressure of the left side of his heart. This would give us a more accurate measurement of how well his heart was tolerating the transfusions and fluids.

During the next three hours, there was a change for the better. James's blood pressure was staying up without the drugs, and the oozing from all his wounds had essentially stopped. He began to regain consciousness and showed no signs of having suffered a stroke. We were able to make him understand the need for the tube in his windpipe. I was still concerned that he had not put out any urine, despite massive amounts of diuretics or "water shots." The filling pressures of his heart chambers continued to rise, reflecting progression of his heart failure. We had visited with Elaine and Phyllis on several occasions, and once again went out to talk with them. After advising them of James's present condition, covering the favorable signs as well as the discouraging ones, I said, "We feel that James is stable enough that we can go home and clean up. We'll be back around six. If you want, we can take you in to see him again before we leave."

This time, Elaine and Phyllis were somewhat encouraged. James was able to respond by nodding his head. Although the tube in his windpipe prevented him from speaking, he was able to squeeze their hands.

I had seen too many cases like this. I knew that it would have been easier for James if he had died in the Emergency Room or in OR. At least, he wouldn't have had to go through the pain and discomfort following surgery. But perhaps there was a reason that we had pulled him through. His family would have some time to prepare themselves for losing him.

20

IT WAS 4:45 A.M. Saturday morning when Sylvia heard the garage door open and met me in the kitchen. As I drank a cup of coffee and ate some cinnamon toast, we talked about James's case and his poor prognosis. When I called the ICU, his condition was about the same.

Somewhat rejuvenated by a warm, relaxing shower, I dressed in a suit and prepared to return to St. John's. As I started to leave, I asked Sylvia to tell Monte how sorry I was that I had missed the rest of his scrimmage and to tell Gary that I would not be able to go to his soccer game. I would be spending most of the day with James.

Julie, looking remarkably refreshed in a clean, white uniform, met me in the ICU a little before six. James had still not put out any urine and the filling pressure of his heart was markedly elevated, despite my earlier order to cut back on his i.v. fluids. The most serious new development was the change in his electrocardiogram, indicating injury to his heart. This was not surprising since his blood pressure had been so low for such a long period of time and his heart was now straining to carry the additional fluid load.

We went to the Waiting Room where Elaine and Phyllis had spent the last ten hours. It had been a long night for them.

"James seems to be about the same," I said, "but he still hasn't had any urine output. I'm worried about his electrocardiogram, too. It shows that he might have suffered a heart attack. If his kidneys don't start to function and help him get rid of the excess fluid, we might have to put him on an artificial kidney machine. I'm not absolutely sure that he's a candidate for it—we'll discuss it later this morning."

We took Elaine and Phyllis into the ICU. "James, it's me," Elaine said softly.

He opened his eyes and nodded.

"Your surgery is over." Elaine went on, "we're waiting outside. Phyllis is with me, and everyone is praying for you. You just get well, so we can take you home."

Julie and I left Elaine and Phyllis and started morning rounds. John told us that he had had his best night since surgery. "Now that I've got my head screwed on right, I know I'll do a lot better," he admitted.

We were overjoyed to see this change. With Bill down the hall unable to have surgery, and James so critically ill in the ICU, I'm not sure I could have tolerated another negative session with John. "I was hoping you would realize that the things I asked of you—such as getting up and walking, coughing, and being pleasant to Mary and the nurses—were ultimately for your benefit."

"I do, Tex. It just took me awhile to recognize how selfish I've been. I'm sorry I've been such a terrible patient."

Julie put her hand on his shoulder. "John, there's no such thing as a terrible patient. But I don't think you were aware of the effect you were having on Mary. We knew that somehow we had to *make* you aware. We refuse to let our patients get well at the emotional expense of those who love them most."

This had been a humbling experience for John, and I felt for him. For the first time I was confident that he would do well.

But what a battle! How difficult it had been attempting to change his attitude after surgery. How much more pleasant it would have been had we—and he—been able to achieve this attitude before surgery. We told John that we would check in again during the evening, and continued rounds.

Carl was eager for Sunday night's pre-op talk. He wanted to know what to expect on Monday morning.

Bill and Deedie were still stunned. They had been so optimistic that surgery could be done to help Bill. Even though we reassured them that medications would make things better, they knew what ultimately lay ahead.

Grace had again gone into atrial fib Friday afternoon, but during the evening had converted back to a regular rhythm. It was encouraging that she had stayed in it for the past twelve hours. The longer she remained in her normal rhythm, the less likely she would be to go back into atrial fib. She had already walked on her own in the hall this morning. It was thrilling to see someone her age so self-sufficient. It was only her third post-op day.

Dick was making amazing progress, too. Having showered and shaved, he met us at the door. With a smirk, he pulled back my coat to see if I was wearing the T-shirt. He kidded us about not wearing our "Smile" T-shirts when we made rounds, and pretended to have hurt feelings. I told him we planned to have them framed to hang in our office.

Shortly after our return to the ICU, James began to deteriorate. His blood pressure dropped, and I had the nurses restart the medications in an effort to stimulate his ailing heart and bring his blood pressure back up to a more normal range. Initially there was some response to these measures, but soon higher rates of administration were necessary to maintain his pressure in the low eighties. I was afraid that he was beginning the long downhill slide. Amazingly, he continued to be fairly alert. After making sure that he was not having a great deal of pain or discomfort, I promised to bring his family back in to see him. I felt the need to talk to Elaine and Phyllis about these recent developments.

"Elaine," I said in the Waiting Room, "James has taken a turn for the worse. His blood pressure has started to fall and he is again needing drugs to stimulate his heart. He still has not put out any urine and the signs of heart failure are more evident. It's just after ten. How well he does during the next four to six hours will determine whether or not we will get him through this. I mentioned earlier that we might consider the artificial kidney machine, but this is now out of the question. It requires a good blood pressure to work properly, and I don't think James's pressure is strong enough for that.

"Because we are having to increase the amount of stimulating drugs, we also have to give him more fluids. As a result, his face and hands will become more puffy, and his lungs will fill with fluid. The greater the amount of fluid in his lungs, the more difficult it will be for him to get oxygen from the lungs into his blood. The less oxygen he gets into his blood, the greater the stress on his heart. The more stress on his heart, the more it fails as a pump, causing more fluid to back up into the lungs. I'm afraid we've entered a vicious cycle."

Phyllis said quickly, "I'm glad that we didn't have to make a decision about using the artificial kidney machine. I don't think he would ever have agreed. We want everything done for my father—up to a point—but he wouldn't want to be kept alive on a machine."

Elaine nodded in agreement.

"We'll take you in to see him again, if you would like."

"I think it would do Daddy good to let him know that we are with him."

Elaine was now able to respond. "I would like to go back in, if you'll go with me."

We knew how close this family was. Their love and compassion made it all the more difficult for them to see James in his present condition. He had never before been a patient in a hospital and had rarely seen a doctor. His last physical exam had been more than five years ago. Illness was a new and devastating experience for the family. Julie and I knew that our role would become a supportive one, directed at helping them cope with what lay ahead. Every thirty to forty-five minutes we visited with Elaine and Phyllis, attempting to keep them informed and preparing them for what now seemed inevitable.

Just before one, James lost consciousness. We brought Elaine and Phyllis in to see him, and as we walked with them back to the Waiting Room, I told them that I felt the end was near. Their reaction indicated that they were ready to accept it.

Upon our return to the ICU, we found that James was terminal. His pulse was irregular and his blood pressure was steadily dropping, despite increased amounts of stimulating drugs. He had fought the good fight, but I could not bear to see his wonderful wife and daughter go through the prolonged hell of watching him die slowly. I discontinued the stimulating drugs. I had tried everything that I knew to prolong James's life; I would not prolong his death.

We stood in the room at James's bedside. Julie held one hand and I held his other. We had never really gotten to know James, but we both felt close to him. We would not let him die alone.

Twenty minutes later his heart developed a fatal irregularity. The fight was over.

I felt the sense of loss, but it was a relief to know that James would not have to suffer any longer. Now came the hardest part. Having to tell Elaine and Phyllis would not be easy, no matter how much I had tried to prepare them for this moment or how well prepared they thought they were.

As we headed toward the Waiting Room, I said to Julie, "I'm

sorry. I know that this has been just as hard on you as it has on me. We did everything we could."

Julie was too upset to speak. We walked the remaining distance of the long corridor in silence.

We had entered the Surgical Waiting Room through the same door numerous times this week. Each time, whether for the families of Walter, John, Grace, or Dick, there had been a smile on our faces. This time we were solemn. Julie sat down beside Phyllis, and put her arm around Phyllis's shoulders. I knelt on the floor beside Elaine, and grasped her hands in mine. "It's all over, Elaine. James passed away a few minutes ago."

"Oh, no," she moaned, burying her head in her lap. "He can't be gone. Not my James. What will I do without him? How can I go on without the man I have lived with the last fifty-three years?"

Tears rolled down Phyllis's cheeks. Mechanically, she attempted to wipe her tears. Most of them rolled unblotted into her lap.

"Phyllis," I said, "I'm sorry. We did everything we possibly could, but we have to accept this as His will."

I got up from my kneeling position and sat beside Elaine. Except for her sobs, the empty Waiting Room was silent. After a few minutes, Elaine was calmer. I felt they were ready to hear what I knew had to be said.

"You were aware that James's chances were very slim. Our goal was to get him through surgery and give him back to you the way he was before he got sick. Neither of you would have wanted him to survive as a bedridden invalid, dependent on a kidney machine for the rest of his life; nor would he have wanted this. As hard as it is for you to accept, he's better off now. He's no longer in pain. He's with the Best Doctor of all now."

"He wouldn't have wanted to live as an invalid," Elaine said emphatically. "He was always very active. He would not have wanted to lie in an Intensive Care Unit for weeks and weeks, struggling to get well, and then still not make it. I know he's better off now than the other way, but it still hurts to give him up."

"Would you like to go back and see James? I recommend that you don't. I think you should remember him the way he was before he got sick, rather than the way he looks now. But I certainly won't keep you from going back in if that is what you want to do. Julie and I will go with you."

After thinking for a moment, Elaine said, "Yes, I would like to see him again. Phyllis, will you go too?"

Phyllis agreed to join us, and the four of us walked slowly to the ICU one last time. After James had expired, Julie and I had helped the nurses remove the tube from his windpipe, along with the other i.v.'s and lines. We had tried to make him look as normal as possible in case his family wanted to make a final visit. I explained to Elaine and Phyllis what we had done and what they should expect to see. I also warned them that James would still look puffy and pale.

As we approached the room, Elaine clutched my arm. She stopped in the doorway. The room was empty except for the body of her husband. He lay on his back with his eyes closed. A fresh white sheet covered all but his face and its peaceful expression.

Recovering from the initial shock, Elaine went to James's side. She asked if she could hold his hand. I took his cold, pale hand from beneath the sheet and placed it in hers. Elaine bent down and kissed his cold cheek. This time her affection would not be returned. Her farewell words were "James, I'll see you in heaven."

I looked at Julie, standing with Phyllis on the opposite side of the bed. A wave of emotion passed between us. Only because Julie and I had allowed ourselves to become so involved with James and his caring family could we fully appreciate the real meaning of Elaine's statement.

Phyllis patted her father's left hand, still covered by the sheet. She bent down and kissed its form. "Good-by, Daddy. You've been a wonderful father. I'll really miss you."

I supported Elaine and Julie gave comfort to Phyllis as we left the ICU. Once in the hall, I said, "I've gotten very close to you over the last eighteen hours. I really didn't get the chance to know James, but I can tell from knowing you that he was a wonderful person. From what I have seen during the last hours of James's life, I could sense that he loved you very much and you both loved him. I know that it is hard for you to give him up, but I hope you will look at it this way. Elaine, you have lost a wonderful husband, and Phyllis, you have lost a wonderful father, but God has gained a wonderful angel." I fought to hold back the tears. The others couldn't, and didn't.

Sunday afternoon Sylvia, Monte, Gary, and I stood on the first tee at the country club. I had been able to catch up on some of the sleep I had lost while taking care of James. For the moment, I was free of the pressures of St. John's.

As I watched my wife and boys make their tee shots, I thought of the other families whose lives had been so closely meshed with mine during the past week. I was grateful that Walter had done exceptionally well and was already home. John's attitude had changed completely. This morning on rounds he had been sincerely cheerful. Grace and Dick continued to show excellent improvement. The thrill of seeing each of them doing so well was further enhanced by the knowledge that I had possibly helped make the trauma of their operations a little easier on Becky, Mary, Charles and Jackie.

But, as gratifying as the results of those four cases were, I continued to agonize over the plight of Bill. He was a courageous patient who would have given anything to have been a candidate for open-heart surgery. Having to turn down someone like Bill is always heartbreaking. And then there was James.

By the time we reached the eighteenth tee, my attention had shifted to the week that lay ahead. In a few hours I would be presenting the pre-op talk to Carl and his family for his open-heart surgery tomorrow morning.

Julie and I are different today from what we were seven days ago. We have been enriched by our association with Walter, John, Grace, and Dick and their families. But Bill and Deedie, and James, Elaine, and Phyllis have left their mark on us, too. By this time next week we will have been affected by Carl and his family, and the other patients after him and their families. That is the price we must pay for the privilege of being in this "field of honor," where the sorrow of the "agony of defeat" serves to constantly remind us of the joy of the "thrill of victory."

Having read this book, possibly you will be different also. If your destiny should be that of James, I pray that you and your family can accept it with dignity. But if you are among the many fortunate ones who come through surgery with an excellent result, as I feel you will be, I hope that you will find the courage and inspiration to lift the burden of suffering from the hearts of those who love you most as often as you can and as cheerfully as possible. If you don't, I hope that there will be someone around who cares enough to "kick your bed!"

Glossary

angina: the sudden onset of chest pain caused by insufficient blood supply to heart muscle; usually subsides quickly with rest or medications.

aorta: the largest artery coming out of the heart; carries oxygen-rich blood to the rest of the body; one end of the bypass grafts are sutured to this.

aorta (abdominal): the continuation of the largest artery coming out of the heart; the portion confined to the abdomen before it divides into the two leg arteries.

arterial blood gases: a test that measures how well oxygen is transferred from the lungs into the patient's blood.

arterial pressure (blood pressure): a direct, mechanical measurement of the pressure in arteries, generated by the force of the heart's contraction.

atrium (right atrium): the filling chamber for the right side of heart; the receiving chamber of the heart for unoxygenated (venous) blood from the upper and lower parts of body.

cardiovascular clinical specialist: a nurse with a master's degree who specializes in blood-vessel–related diseases.

cardiovascular surgery: a subspecialty confined to operations on the heart and major blood vessels.

coronary arteries: the small vessels that supply blood to the heart; they are the first blood vessels to branch off of the aorta.

coronary arteriograms: see *heart catheterization.*

coronary artery bypass graft (bypass graft): a surgical procedure in which a segment of vein is taken from the leg, then one end is connected to the aorta and the other end is sewn to a blocked heart artery, thereby delivering the blood supply to the blocked artery beyond the blockage.

coronary artery disease: hardening of the heart arteries; the development of blockages in the heart arteries; almost always present in heart attacks.

electrocardiogram: the tracing of electrical activity of heart; used to reveal rhythm and heart rate as well as possible injury or death of the heart muscle.

flow-by oxygen: a supply of oxygen connected to a plastic breathing tube; the patient breathes on his or her own, as opposed to a *respirator*, which breathes for the patient.

fibrillation: state of electrical and mechanical chaos of the heart; quivering of heart muscle so that it no longer functions as a pump. If of the ventricles or pumping chambers, it is fatal unless corrected by shocking the patient. If of the atria or filling chambers, it causes a rapid, irregular pumping action of the ventricles and is not lethal.

heart attack (myocardial infarction): acute death of the heart muscle caused by blockages in the heart arteries; usually associated with chest pain that may radiate into neck, jaws, or arms; often accompanied by nausea and cold, clammy sweat.

heart catheterization (heart cath; cath): a procedure where movies are taken of the coronary arteries as dye is injected into these arteries; used to show blockages in the heart arteries.

heart-lung machine (the pump): specialized equipment that completely takes over the pumping function ot the heart as well as the lungs so that a patient's heart can be completely stopped.

heart sac: tough, fibrous tissue surrounding the heart, separating it from the lungs.

hypo: a shot given to the patient for pain or prior to surgery; usually contains a narcotic.

left ventricle (left ventricular pumping function): the main pumping chamber of the heart; how well it contracts or empties is an index of how damaged the heart is from previous heart attacks.

medical management: treatment of heart pain (*angina*) using medications.

nitroglycerine: special medication that temporarily allows an increased flow of blood through the heart arteries by causing them to dilate; placed under the tongue for relief of angina.

preinfarction angina: chest (heart) pain that persists much longer than usual; no evidence of heart attack on electrocardiogram or blood tests. See *angina.*

respirator: a mechanical breathing machine that is used only to pump air into a patient's lungs; it cannot take over the pumping function of the heart.

treadmill: a machine with a conveyor belt that the patient walks on while he or she is connected to an electrocardiogram; the machine may be elevated and the conveyor speed increased to stimulate increased work for the patient's heart. This test is designed to show acute changes in the electrocardiogram if blockages in heart arteries are present.